# kHarLaMoV's

# aNkLe

a utopian fantasy

by robert majzels

THE ELEPHANTS

Gravestone with woman at the door to the other world.
Photo by Robert Majzels, Chengdu, April 2009.

Illustration on page 59: Antonin Artaud, “Lettre sort autographe signée à Hitler Chancelier du Reich,” in *Works on Paper*, edited by Margit Rowell. The Museum of Modern Art: Distributed by H.N. Abrams, 1996, pp. 50-51. Original work housed in Bibliothèque nationale de France – Département des manuscrits.

Illustration on page 112: “Talisman to repair damage where calamity has struck and to destroy a ghost devil or human destructor,” “道教符咒 [Daojiao fuzhou] (Daoist Magic Incantations),” Chinese Fengshui Research Society, May 23, 2017.

18 19 20 21 22 5 4 3 2 1

***



Distributed by Small Press Distribution, Inc.

Printed in Canada

***

The Elephants Ltd.
theelephants.net

ISBN 978-1-988979-31-1 print
ISBN 978-1-988979-32-8 e-book

Produced by Moveable Inc.
moveable.com

Edited by Broc Rossell

Cover design by Shanna Compton. Cover art is a derivative work collaging and adapting two photos: “sky story” by @ichsxn on Unsplash and “Everyone gets a window” by pedrik on Flickr, licensed under CC BY 2.0.

ACKNOWLEDGEMENTS

My thanks to the Canada Council for the Arts, whose financial support made the writing of this work possible, and to the writers who, through their jury service, help to feed their fellows and occasionally make room for the production of less orthodox writing.

I am grateful to the first reader of *kHarLaMoV's aNkLe*, Claire Huot; her encouragement, her insights, and her knowledge of China and Chinese were indispensable.

If you are reading this book, you can blame Erín Moure: she convinced the idjit not to toss the thing into the ethereal fog, and then guided it in the direction of publication. Also, while I'm at it, my gratitude for the pleasure of her poetry over the years.

A huge thanks to Joe Kotler for his generous sharing of Moveable Inc.'s resources, and especially to Jim Roberts for his unparalleled reading and proofreading skills, and to Isabel Preto for her assiduous typesetting.

Finally, thanks to Broc Rossell and Jordan Scott for their courage and commitment to challenging the limits of literature.

Excerpts from this work were published by The Chicago Review, filling Station and Touch the Donkey.

after we lit up harpeR we lay low for a. while diNO did a backdoor rip copped a gram we. got strung out pretty bad meanwhile. very mean. mean as all fucking get. out in the street they're marching jogging hiking cycling in honour of some fallen police. a fallen po. lice not a week goes by they're. not commemorating past glorious barbarisms pouring another heroic gangster's anglogermanish name into the history books people tightrope-walking ironmanning climbing freefalling to raise money for pharmaceutically sanctioned diseases why not nationalize the fucking pharmabastards where the fuck do you think all that money goes go ahead gather together exercise our prejudices pray to the dOW build fences and lay turf down to fill the dead zones between ourselves and our neighbours (neighbors if I'm looking to break into the aMeriCan market (ha)) gargle. herbicides and pesticides and sweeten it all with turquoise-flavoured mouthwash. the world is full of bad poets but you're not one of them we may think the situation the people the whole damned planet the urgency all of it requiring immediate action on a global scale we might yet squeeze through a very narrow window only we got to act now hurry. hurry hang on a minute while i make another buck meanwhile who. will prepare the fish? emily carr wants to know for the terrible journey ahead

but the story was supposed to be about how we did that shit harper meanwhile we got strung out strung out pretty bad that's the hard nut being. hooked on this shit not unlike carrying a mortgage all the work the daily grind dealing ripping give us this day our daily running down the dope copping watch out the pigs just so you can get off and start all over again might as well nine-to-five it the kids. the car the job diNO does a backdoor job this next part. is true you know it is by the *realist* narrative style of the writing how this works diNO brings the buyer in the front door of the frat house shall we pause here to describe diNO a blade of uncut grass tall rake-thin a bit of fuzz on the upper lip bell bottoms for shit's sake how to write diNO without turning him into just another fucking noun in dresses diNO? are you still out there man so he sits the kid down in the front room on account of he tells him the seller's shy mean. while we're downstairs in the basement in the kitchen eating noodles that's all we got diNO long-legs-it downstairs big hurry out the back door and gone gone gone no big deal not the first time we know the routine wait a while then one of us wingbends

to bear and not to own
to act and not lay claim
to do the work and
let it go

老子 (laozi)

a knee upstairs. to the front room talk the yokel down go ahead man pissandmoan get it off your nipples how he'll kill the motherfucker we're very sympathetic not our problem also scare the yokel just a bit how diNO's been known to carry a piece end of discussion go home and freak out kid you been ripped end of story when i write dow i mean dOw not dAo pray to the dOW joNeS and who will prepare the fish for the terrible journey ahead well those noodles weren't actual noodles more like kraFt plastic diddles without that orange powdered napalm we had no idea how to cook a noodle

we were in a murky room in a murky basement of a murky. frat house we were in the citY of the wRongfully dEad upstairs on saturday night the murky frat boys drinking kegs of pissy beer watch porn flicks in surround sound occasionally bring in a couple of unsuspecting girls occasionally a frat boy deepsixes on bended knee to collect. the rent for our murky room toilet shower stall just enough clothes to sit in the laundromat half naked in canned lit the atwoods were always. a nuclear family we were the gangs of marauding boys and girls the bit of grit in the national literature imagine the oyster's surprise a bit of grit irritating at first then tonguing and. tonguing it that tiny bit of grit wrenched from the hunchback of unhappiness the oyster working it smooth. glossy and perfectly round but we can't even eat those oysters any more we were deadlining boot it baby boot it who wouldn't prefer booting it to a weekend up at the cottage cheese we watched the red orchid. spread her legs life can be beautiful but not for long the weeks go by better get your game uptight go see. the old man

connaître le dao est
facile ne pas en parler
est difficile

庄子 (zhuangzi)

that old mAn mostly you couldn't get a word out of the grizzly. bAstArd tight as a clam which is a mixed animal metaphor why go see him if that's how he's going to do no idea why that old man laboUred along the dao a twice trackless way through the forest of illusions no clear path forward no trail behind to follow. the old man's way no and he spoke little wrote even less most people breathe with their throats but the old man breathed with his heels when he did speak he said with all the confusion in the world these days assuming we knew the way to change it no matter how often we point the way what good would it do and if we know it does no good and still make ourselves do it this too is a kind of confusion so it is best to leave things alone and not force them if we don't force things at least we won't cause anyone any worry we cast a small stone into the ballot box in lieu of an illusion after the election the war the bombs the killing continued when he wrote he tossed everything he wrote quickly before the corpse was cold the writing. not the written silent yes mostly but hip to the planet the politics the pigs he practiced a kind. of dirty daoism a dAdA dAoist is the one sweeping. the stairs you walk by on your way into the temple a daDa daOist will off a pig bust up the reactionary radio what kind of daoist is that a dada daoist is what kind we were not his followers no such thing as daoJiaotu he had no followers he would not strive a daOist is going nowhere long ago he'd turned away from excellence and the slick language of success he was withdrawn preferred to cut himself off occasionally bemused he forgot what he was going to say and yet because he regarded wisdom as what is timely there were things that he could not keep from doing

henceforth together
we'll trace our dream of
the peony pavilion
汤显祖 (tang xianzu)

because he'd learned true words aren't beautiful he chose reticence he used knots instead of writing

scene one LEGEND *by busy world rejected in my own world of retreat. i pondered a hundred schemes. finding joy in none* his name was 胡波 (huBO in pinyin) young tall slim wiry muscles long hair pulled back in a bun puts his left foot forward bends the knee leans into the note E3 behind him niK morGaN older shorter but still. fit blue eyes blond hair not quite shoulder length now gripping hubo's right arm pulling him back the other way lean into it pull nik shouts hubo rises to E4 niK pulls harder shouts now hit the E5. hUbO throws all his weight forward pitches his voice up into his head hits E5 morgan pulls him into a bear hug applause all round a very surprising way to teach singing huBO tells nik but i can see the balance of projecting and restraint the pulling back and forward at once huBO nikOlas morgAn and a half dozen chinese singing students in a workshop in the bEijing centrAl coNservatory of mUsic nik morGan wEstern countertenor brought in by the kanadian embassy to collaborate with huBO china's premier performer of dan 旦 female roles in the mei lanFang peKing oPeRa troupe also present seated at the back of the classroom in a dark blue skirt'n'jacket clAIre nOmI kaNadian cultural attaché in china the idea was hers i mean bringing the countertenor to beiJing not all this writing about it

idjit that's a nickname idjit did the dreaming. for all of us his thing he was the aNkLe's dreamer idjit dreamed we quit naTo withdrew all our country's troops from outside its borders turned. CF18s into ploughshares turned management shares into ploughshares turned the oil patch into a garden patch burned the whole thing down meanwhile that mean wily motherfucker pharaOh fucking harper would not let the people go there was resistance but any resistance will bog down a minor. momentary occupation peters out a few hundred or a thousand why not in the street on a sunny sunday afternoon then it all falls quiet in a democracy protest is tolerated so long. as it doesn't disrupt the dAILY commute to work and leisure oh yes we sympathize we really do excuse me while i make another buck notice how this. form allows for the occasional rant more or less and the less the better

whenever the mouth opens
and the tongue moves
disaster is close behind

河上公 (heShang gong)

what's eerie ethereal asexual ambiguous androgynous disembodied slippery fishlike and yet breathes from the heels not from the throat come on old man give us the word let's do some damage break some glass do some shattered window shopping pour molasses all over rushhour beef up their national security soft targets take down one. of the bastards because this ain't yer litter-at-church this ain't. yer canned lit this don't ride yer curse sillyassbus this ain't yer indigo teddy bears and coffee mugs this ain't yer well wrought urn this don't make a fucking poem this ain't. yer pay to enter write-a-haiku-'n'-rip-off-another-culture-in-blissful-ignorance contest we had. no. ambition we dulled our edges and did not insist on anything we did not care about beauty we softened our light and forgot about ourselves satUrday the stupid frat boys held their usual my poem is bigger than your poem reading in the street sparkle mOtion on blades shouldered her way past the stupid frat boys debbie carried a long sharp measuring stick on one edge. of that stick she measured terror on the other delight elisA saMpedrin hit the road searching for a language in which to write cabbage and really mean it bobby 2shoes we called him that on account of one of his shoes was red the other merely brown who will prepare the fish for the terrible journey ahead radioactive sea song oil slick down your hair

then you must be one of those
who broaden their learning
in order to ape the sages heaping
absurd nonsense on the crowd
plucking the strings and singing
sad songs all by yourself in hopes
of buying fame in the world

庄子

"I called clarke over to the bench, looked over at kharlamov and said I think he needs a tap on the ankle" that was a direct quote he was unarmed but appeared to be resisting we shot him twice in the face police are still searching for a motive for the attack haha the police searching for a motive the state dEpartMent apologized for the unintentional loss of life this is the way to harvest radishes

scene two DECLARING AMBITION *young scholar drilling the wall for light by which to study. hair tied to a beam to prevent drowsing* after the class cLaire nOmi treats mOrgan and huBO to beijing noodles in a sAnlitun neighbourhood eatery a bit of local colour for morGan's benefit claire and hubo jabbering away in mAnDariN while mORGAN takes in the imperial crimson ceiling trimmed in gold red tablecloths sullen. waiters in black and white loud clatter of voices dishes trucks & carts. in the beijINg street now you may be thinking we've introduced something like another entirely different narrative entirely different setting or pretense of a setting on the opposite side of the planet in the heart of the mysteriosa oRient as the white folks like to say also quick sketch of characters niKolas morGan countertenor hubO peking opera dAN claire noMi cultural attaché kanadian embassy all seemingly loaded up for a long plod i meant plot we can hope somehow the writer will find a way to dovetail these two stories that so far couldn't have less in common or at least solder a lumpy join but that's far from certain considering the author's track record isn't that a kind of tension

a motet to be sung as a round: the language machine dark entered the room in dust in dust the small machine entered my throat

breath

first someone said no more poetry after. AUSC-WITZ then poetry only if. it's broken then poetry because of AUSC-WITZ then poetry in spite of then back to poetry forget AUSC-WITZ

we do not permit our nuns to sing we absolutely forbid it preferring with the bLesSed viRgiN to hymn indirectly in a spirit of humility rather than with heRoD's notorious daughter to pervert the minds of the weak with lascivious strains (saInt giLbeRt of sempringHam c.1100)

but we were storytelling harper how we planned to light the stupid bastard up so this is how narrative did harper in catch him where he wasn't. surrounded by the rOyal kanadiAn money police the seesicks exmilitary thugs so in a place he felt tight yer maybe thinking but how would i know what yer thinking any more than you could guess what i'm thinking as though what i was thinking was or were what i'm writing the old man said do you know the taste of 甘露 *ganLu* the sweet dew of meditation when you press your tongue against the roof of your mouth it is the emptiness at its centre that makes a wheel work existence makes a thing useful but nonexistence makes it work which reminds me king john sporting black cape and handlebar whiskers why we called him kIng jOhn in those days you could get away with a getup like that we thought ok cool for a while till we found out he was dealing acid for saTan's choICE only he had no choice in the end had to roll up the cape and thumb his ass out of. town or they'd have owned him. for life. which would have been a short time

strangers in the crowd we'd have felt that anyway only the smack in our veins gave us a reason for our difference we lived at night at dawn searching for a place to crash shuffling against the flow of showered caffeinated smudgeheads on the dAilY commute we did not write about the city we wrote on the city tous ceux qui se sont concertés pour m'empêcher de prendre l'héroïne tous ceux qui ont touché à aNNe maNson à cause de cela le dimanche mai 1939 je les brûlerai vivants sur une place de paris et je leur ferai perforer et brûler les moëlles (antOnin artAud SORT #6)

and yet not yet was our motto we lived. in chrOnic readiness except. when we lay in undivided stillness the frat house where we rented rooms being close by the university we occasionally shouldered an academic off the curb occasionally entered the academy to use the washroom meanwhile the old man lived a long way away stayed clear of the conservatory made his own temple in the east a 1½ out by the oil refineries not exactly working first impressions still he never raised anyone's rent something not all of us can say he made simple music out of sticks and string here a thot from littLe waLter B the destructive character lives. from the feeling not that

the mind is one if someone
knew it there would be two
going from one to two is
the origin of all delusion

苏辙 (su zhe)

life is worth living but that suicide is not worth the trouble everyone seeks happiness to be incomplete is to become whole we would not dig deeper we would not calculate we would not seek to be whole similarly but differently stated by sKiP jAmEs i'm so glAd i'M so glad i'm glAd i'm gLad i'm glad i'm so glad i'm so glad i'm glad i'm glad i'm glad

but harPer yes you may be thinking in church not that we ever did much thinking in. there all the incense going to your head nevertheless haRper you're thinking every sunday in the chriStian and miSSionary alliance church no less we thought of that too sure but. after the kKk. sent that halfwit stooge boy with a bowl haircut into cHarLestoN's eMmaNueL afRiCan metHodiSts houSe of pRaYer we got jittery dragged our asses to the old man for a consult he thought on it a while as was his way we knew to sit quiet and wait could be he said after cHarLestoN the white folks might just tighten up their own places of warshit how narrative trickles along the same well. worn synaptic highways first we bomb the hell out of their towns then we welcome them with open arms first armaments then arms why we say of history's lessons nothing. remains but the occasional pop in the dark'n'derelict fields of the hippocampus and the fish their lidless eyes turned inward dreaming of a way back

traité sur l'extase
qui consiste à s'asseoir
et perdre conscience
司馬承禎
(sima chengzhen)
*questions to heaven*

that last bit edging toward the lyrical can we cut that insidious artful shit creeping back in after we swore we wouldn't do that on account. of this ain't yer litter-rah-rah-ry press sucking off the state's tit acts just like a big press only smaller this ain't reading in yer shithole town tonight this ain't. yer artsyfartsy goody-two-shoes creeeeAtif writhing grad-you-it stewed.ent meanwhile. hackademics jerk off another critterical paper at one another for performance points in the annual review we were emilianO's bandits on smack booger junior says you drop. the bombs we'll locate targets refuel yer killing machines our dirty oil hELLo i'm bob and i'm a poet hello bob i haven't written a poem in 24 hours some folks would say longer those marShall islanders shall we welcome them with open arms my idea any idea is a sponge only a sponge in a tsunami well…

scene three ADMONISHING THE DAUGHTER *a virtuous and eligible young lady has always needed an understanding of letters so that when the time comes for her to marry a learned husband she will not be deficient in conversation* think of clAire nOmi her years in revolutionary cHinA during the cultural revolution and the aftermath and chairman mAO gone but westerners still rare her fluent mAndArin reading and writing chiNese opening doors and smart pretty so nIKolas mOrgan wants to somehow let her know he's neither castrated nor particularly gay (not that he has anything…) because you don't have to be castrated or gay to sing countertenor the high voice being a technique not a condition or sexual preference a point ordinarily he's tired of making

an aleXandrine is a line of twelve syllables — sometimes divided in.to two equal phrases — by a break called a cAE.sura between the sixth — and seventh syllables. and sometimes into. three — four-syllable. sections by two. caesuras and — geNeRaL aToMicS. is the maker of the — pREDator drone

check out the chriStian and miSSionary aLLianCe that bastard harPer's fave outfit the fulfillment of tHe gReaT coMMiSSion aggressive evan–gelism think ciA with a bible in their back pockets those missionaries born again and again. and again church planting around the globe spreading the cash around plugging the odd interference in maMou guiNea weSt aFrica some minor abuse in the C&MA church over there bit of psychological abuse excessive beatings touch of sadistic dental practices performed without novocaine sexual molestation rape oops shall we. move on eMilY dicKinson and the iDjit volunteered to go in on a sunday the fiRst alliAnce cHurch off deerfooT

the dao is like water
people are like fish

庄子

trAil in southeast cAlVary alBerty emily D had one or two dark ankle-length frocks but idjit needed a suit so he ripped off some uptown high-end concession shop in mardaloopy

we did not like harper we named him all-the-tiny-white-people dropping bombs all-the-tiny-white-people droning songs all-the-tiny-white-people fuck the dog the machine dark entered the room in dust in dust the small machine entered my throat some boys played hockey broke #kharlamovsankle others joined the army dropped some bombs. from a very great height all-the-tiny-white-people elections came and went pimp pendulum of hope nothing changed except as a rough indication of the shifting relations of power between factions of the ruling class

to be like water bringing help
to all without competing

庄子

the words of the holy spirit should not be sung in soft broken voices in a somewhat womanish manner but uttered with manly sounds and feelings YES indeed it is seemly for men to sing in manly voices and not to ape. as it were the wantonness of actors with shrill or false voices used in an effeminate manner (sainT bernarD of clairvauX 1090–1153)

breath

my life a penny i've held between my knees waiting for the perfect moment to let it go the moment that might give it meaning or value until looking back i can see not one but several of those moments i let them pass my knees shaking but tightly squeezed together now weak-kneed broken forgotten time has come to swallow that penny

scene four THE PEDANT'S LAMENT *seven reasons why i'll bite & scratch for an academic post* reason 1 to have something to brag about to my family friends & neighbours reason 2 for the chance of a bribe or two in exchange for a flattering review reason 3 to hitch my wagon to a rising star reason 4 for a chance at government or private funding reason 5 to puff myself up and eventually trade up for a better position reason 6 to lord it over my inferiors (more recent hirees sessionals tAs students) reason 7 to obtain sexual favours from female students but worse than all of these what mencius said the worst human vice is the urge to teach others

grabbed a wheelchair out front — the salVation aRmy turned up sunday mass firsT alLiance church emilY — diCkInson decked out in a very plain & exquisitely clean white pique & a blue net worsted shawl idjit in his dichlorobenzene suit — pushing behind they made a place for her in the aisle so that when the sleepy service done people filing out haRper had to come her way pausing every politician's reflex — before a child or disabled body the moment she might have smiled to reassure him we'd suggested that but emiLy D had long ago stopped smiling she reached into the folds of that blue net worsted shawl — here's where she would have produced the dark oiled machine of her throat pointed to his lowbrow and pulled a perfect round — entry wound is what they call it — only we had no such weapon anyway emilY D was not a fan of the full stop she preferred the — dash so what she drew from the folds of her blue net worsted shawl was an astute perceptive garden blade leaned forward and up and drew her long dash across — the bastard's throat

how 朱耷 zhuDa became 八大山人 baDa shanRen if you were born zhuDa in the city of naNchang in 1626 and a prince of the yiYang branch of the mINg imperial family you'd study philosophy politics painting sounds a fine life until the manCHu come down from the north that was the end of those imperial miNG how should one act. when the mANchu come down from the north is an enduring question the mANchu are forever and again coming down from some north or other how should we act some will offer their services grease the wheel provide the information ease the transition excuse me while i make another buck some take up the gun take to the hills zhuDa put on a monk's robes took. refuge in the

the comma is like a man
holding the door open
for you i'll take a breath
when i please

gertrude stein

temple later even the temple was too much tore his robes walked the streets feigned or didn't feign madness in the end born prince zhuDa like him you might choose to become a hermit with an ink brush painting small animals a bird a fish among lotus roots on the edge of an empty space bada shanren homeless we no longer feared cataSTROPHE we lived right in the heart of it we did not look to the future fuck that we lived in the present the unspeakable present not. denying that any real struggle for change is waged in among and by communities everyone remembers the panthers' guns but their power was rooted in breakfast programs health clinics schools only we had no community no health no school and we generally skipped breakfast we were kharlamov's ankle we served the occasional need. for violence because protest is tolerated so long as the daily commute hang on while i make another buck mean. while mornings the hackademics retweet a friend's progressive cat video hit the treadmill for a five mile jog then off to school show off how smart they are later a drink with a hated colleague and home to bed the peaceful transition to fascism

and your name shall
no longer be אברם (abram)
but your name shall be
אברהם (abraham) for
i have made you the father
of a multitude of nations

בראשית (bereishit) 17:5

in the confusion that followed idjit got away they locked emIly D away in a cell rest of her life how the morons thought to punish a recluse

scene five ENGAGING THE TUTOR *let her read what she should read if she falls short of the standard beat her maidservant* they're in cLaire noMi's office at the embASSy he in the visitor's chair she armed with a desk here a bit of exposition concealed as dialogue — how's the workshop going? not too exhausting for you morGan smiling shrugs — bit of jet lag ask me in a couple of weeks — by then your mAndarin should be pretty good — yours seems better than pretty good — well I've been at it for a while... how're you getting along with huBO — alright he's great in the workshops a bit tough on the students but not a lot tougher than we had it back home he and i haven't had a drink yet and we haven't talked about the performance — well he won't say much until we've settled everything with the officials — i thought that was all set before i agreed to come — it was and will be this is just the way things work here chInese officials like to leave a doubt hanging over our heads just to be sure we appreciate what they're giving us — i thought we were the ones doing the giving they're not paying me — sure only it's not every day they allow a foreign country's embassy to hold a concert in china let alone in the fOrbIddEn cIty this is a big step they're still recovering from the cultural revolution maO's only been gone a half dozen years they're still wary of dealing with western countries — why are they doing it then — because it's not every day you get a countertenor and a pEking opEra dan on the same stage they like the idea impressed by the idea i'd like to think. it has that eAst meets west ping-pong diplomacy cachet anyway let me worry about that side of things you enjoy the workshop are you walking around a bit i'll see if i can get us into the concert hall just to check it out

happiness is a warm gun

john lennon

we'd have loved to slit his throat who wouldn't. i mean allegedly. or put a nail in him only an unregistered firearm costs bread we took the bus out. to the motel strip on the road out of town to see diNO's guy naPoLi owned a motel out there and a garage next door strolled into the office diNO told naPoLi what we were looking for sure naPoLi big grizzly sitting back behind a cluttered desk says you boost me a 2015 honda civic white if you can but any colour if you can't my guy can do the paint you bring that buggy in and i'll give you a piece clean never been fired reached into a drawer handed diNO the slim jim that's noir for how-to-steal-a-car

— let's paint a picture of the world right now — that's mi$ter roNNie ep$tein bAnk of aMeriKa analyst talking to forTune magaZine (september 13, 2014) — you've got the euroPeans worried about what the ruSSians are doing in their backyard we've got our hands full right now in iraQ you've got the isRaelis with their hands full in their region and then you have the cHiNeSe and jaPaNeSe in the sOutH cHinA seA as an investor with this much regional conflict in the world at least from a sentiment point of view that can't be bad — end of quote meanwhile if that ain't mean enuff idjit dreamed the aNkle rounded up all the minor social parasites lawyers accountants notaries real estate agents financial advisers condo managers fund managers botox quacks developers hedge and dropped them down a shithole

but if anything can further strengthen the deTERMination — indeed the peace of mind — with which i think of my inTENTion, it must be the shrewd dignified use to which i put my last days or weeks (little walter B) whereas locKheed marTin producer of the hellFire miSSile

a word here about the old man's dog that dog. wasn't HIS dog he did not teach the dog to fetch beg sit or roll over he learned more from the dog than he could teach a dog if he ever thought to teach a dog anything if someone wanted to be done with artifice and other. reactionary forms of reader manipulation our teachers call craft then the present tense would not be an imaginary no-time but rather two simultaneous nows the now of my writing and the now of you reading. happily. once the reader has withdrawn. her suspended gaze the writer can finally abandon all that crafty birdshit with which we litter the page

wasps don't sting him beasts don't claw him birds of prey don't carry him off seal the opening close the gate dull the edge untie the tangle soften the light join the dust

老子

we spotted the 2015 cIvIc in the lot beHinD the municipal courthoUse she's [*sic*] buried. deep and a ways from the building those spots by the door being reserved for the high-end shYsters we went in late morning when the bastards were all in there buying and selling. law & order not to mention justice which you won't get in any courthouse the civic was green not white but the year was right so we slim-jimmied the door jammed the screwdriver into the starter and took her out of there none of us had paper bobby 2shoes took the wheel tho he hadn't done any more driving than the rest of us anyway he improvised nicked a buick turning the corner of walKeR and sAiNt-jaCquEs we fled the scene ground the gears all the way to naPoLi's garage hey diNO are you? still out there we were free radicals we wrote on that wall. pull all the troops out now back door this motherfucker napoli took the honda green and pulled a dark plastic bundle out of the wall unwrapped the piece battleship grey slick smelling of oil very heavy very real let's lay that burner down on the desk

breath

idJit osCaR curly jOe miKe wIrTh we sometimes called red mike & jUdy jUdy bobby 2shoes emiLy dIckInsOn little jimmy little eMily cArr neeDles jAkE diNO all gone without a trace not even google could. find them now

reasons why we hate shakesPeare: the inability to combine tragedy and comedy in the same scene

meanwily those kaNaDiaNs poured $15 billion into munitions and spent a pleasant weekend hiking in the mountains didn't wang cHEn say an army of 100,000 will give rise to a million refugees on the road

get rid of wisdom and
reason and people will live
a hundred times better

老子

he said that in 809 CE meanwhile. we carried that pistol from naPoLi's motel wrapped in a dark plastic bundle rode the crosstown bus in the rain back. to our attic in the frat house washroom at the end of the hall 20 bucks a week where we had some back&forth about where to stash the thing until diNO went out and copped some scag we got off dumped the piece down by the window forgot about it lay around listening to perry como or andy williams or maybe was black sabbath makes no diff when you're high on skag somebody ordered hawaiian pizza which don't try this at home a complete fuckup on account of no one was hungry on the smack bobby 2shoes scarfed it down anyway & puked out the window onto the lower mansard later we crashed then in the morning idjit figures he better stash the piece up on the roof by the chimney but overnight rain turned to ice so idjit crawls out onto the slope of the lower roof hits the skids down to the edge hanging on there for his measly life dark bundle goes over down 4 floors into the yard do not try any of this shit at home

scene six DESPAIRING HOPES *care not if those in office be not bright care only for the skill with which you write care not for an official's unjust earnings care only for the mastery of your learning* and so it goes east meets west in a male high voice in a forbidden city all that back and forth of race and. gender also plot a hint of possible trouble with the cHiNeSe side of the deal possibly something romantic brewing between nik moRgaN and cLaiRe nOMi a bit. of character development cLaiRe attractive bright creative mind fully bilingual anglish and mandarin mOrgan uncastrated hetero bit of pride re his musical skill plus a bit of hysterical context via terms to google go ahead countertenor peKing oPera dan character beiJing conservatory of mUsic fOrbIddEn cItY culturAl rEvolution ping pong... all in all material for a blockbuster only but however meanwhile what is all this shit doing here where is this shit going and how is it linked with the boys and girls in kHarLaMoV's aNkLe

il éprouvait cette paix que
donne la vie en se retirant
cette tranquillité de l'abandon
au crime et à la mort

maurice blanchot

with the large suitcase on his knees little waLTer B drove wee ping / through the dar ken ing streets to the station with no way out he wrote / i have no other choiçe but to end it... here in a little village / in the pyrenEEs where no one knows me my life reaches its con / clusion slightly pathetic you may think i have no idea what you might think and yet throughout his short life little waLteR never raised anyone's rent

fish prefer deep water yet fish are. stilled with nameless simplicity meanwhile and a very mean while it was. we've left idjit hanging by his fingernails dangling. from the roof hanging on the gutter's edge because when you find yourself in the gutter you may think i have no idea... that's as far as you're gonna fall and yet not yet below the gutter there's still a long way down idjit took a deep breath bent his elbows hooked a leg up on the edge & straining every atrophied muscle in his body crawled up onto the shingles lay there for a bit careful not to look down at his death waiting wide-mouthed anyone's death is an open-mouthed whale waiting idjit crabbed his way back up to the window tossed himself into the room bobby 2shoes went down and fetched the peashooter in the yard crawled out the window a helluva lot more carefully than idjit scrambled over and up to the top roof laid the burner by the brick chimney up there long as it stayed up there that Old pistOl was a perfect. tOOl because a perfect tOOl has nO use

virtue appears
when the way is lost
kindness appears
when virtue is lost

老子

scene seven THE SCHOOLROOM *droning verses revising lines composed last spring what a deadly thought but when i'm through i'll be able to teach the parrot to order tea* her day off clAIRe's going to the forBIDden cITy would mORgan like to string along haven't you been there nuff times all your guests coming over oh sUre she says i only want to see this one inkbrush painting they've got in the palace museum thought you might be interested okay sure tho he's really more interested in her than an inkbrush painting her bright yellow sweater red pleated skirt red sandals they take a yellow polski fiat cab through the wider streets carpeted in blue and khaki riders on flying pigeon bicycles

justice appears
when kindness is lost
ritual appears
when justice is lost

老子

occasional donkey-drawn carts laden with coal or vegetables come in from the countryside to the back gate north entrance on jingshan road early morning so too early for the crowds cept a few groups of peasants from distant provinces trickling in squatting in the shade we'll wait here a bit cLaiRe says until a young woman in blue zhongshan jacket blue pants steps out from a small door in the wall a few metres west

ritual marks the waning of belief
and the onset of confusion

老子

of the entrance introduces herself wAng qi shakes hands praises cLaiRe's mandarin leads the way through the small gate and they're backstage in the fORbidden cITy an area tourists never see a row of sheds and offices a few abandoned stone lions in a grassy corner male workers in blue overalls a couple blue-skirted. women a younger man in grey on a black bicycle let's foLLow wAng qi into a larger building a hallway office doors elevator down to a floor below an air-conditioned

augury is the flower of the way
and beginning of delusion

老子

gallery large central table two curators wearing white cotton gloves and white surgical masks hand out gloves and masks unroll a scroll maybe a yard long on the table the inkbrush painting of a broken and dying plum tree all crooked roots bare branches under a text written in the reclusive artist baDa sHanRen's idiosyncratic calligraphy what remains of that once exalted plum tree a broken hollowed-out gaping trunk the roots exposed the branches twisted bare but for a half-dozen

thus we choose thick over thin
the fruit over the flower

老子

desiccated dark smudges the inscription reads they say the earth is never thinner than the sky meanwhile this old monk paints plum blossoms he must learn to be like the brothers boYi and sHuQi to turn his back on power and privilege retreat into the mountains eat fiddleheads and grass until hunger kills him a line of twelve syllables I [*sic*] shall be a bestselling writer after kharlamov each of my books will be on the bestseller lists of LAT NYT PW WP etc my novels will go onto the above lists whether publishers push them hard or not whether I'm pAID a big advance. or not. whether I ever win another award. or not. this is my life I write bestselling novels my novels go onto the bestseller lists on or shortly after publication my novels each travel up to the top and they stay on top for months at least two each of my novels does this so be it see to it I will find the way to do this meanwhile nortHrop gruMman raYtheon churns out more tomaHawk missiles because weapons are a non-renewable resource and highly lucrative

time to time curly joe came up with the rent on time could be. we relied too much on the kid cards was how he made the bread the friday night game upstairs those frat boys were not your top-of-the-line poker brainiacs curly joe on the other hand well you never knew what joe was holding in that other hand back in high school daze curly was a numbers. wizard he was as surprised as anyone on account of aside from numbers and his hair curly didn't have much going not where it counts in high. school which is on the field and binge drinking at the sock hop or whatever they're calling that crap these days reason he never took. up the drinking was the lousy ratio between pleasure & prestige on one hand and the headsplitting puke parade that followed on the other anyway joe might've made it as an international egghead only he forgot. to conceal his talent from the teacher rule being never show your high school algebra teacher yer smarter than he is any high school algebra teacher is always gonna be a bitter s.o.b long story. longer teacher found a way to flunk curly's ass bad penmanship or some such horseshit curly stopped pissing away his

he saw the fists growing at
the recapitulation of the heroic
deeds which they had achieved
they were larger than the man
to whom they belonged

elias canetti

life in skool and hitched his wagon to the poker pony where he could. figure the odds and less the other players thought of him the better still he had to ride a steep learning curve specially when he got into the local small-time hoods' games took on a couple of beatings and a job. packing groceries to pay back what he owed by the time we were kharlamov's aNkLe those hoods came round the frat house looking for him curly joe learned the back door from diNO we sold those hoods some smack & they got too lazy to bother with curly which is when he discovered. the frat boys' friendly friday night game the frat boys were a lazy man's lunch curly joe gobbled em up

the caterpillar bends in order to straighten itself

吴澄 (wu cheng)

in the collection of essays entitled huaiNanZi (139 bce) iLLumination once asked nONExistence if it existed or not nOneXisteNce made no response so unable to perceive any sign of its existence iLLumination sighed i too do not exist but i cannot equal the nonexistence of noNexiStenCe according to c. bOOKer there are only 7 basic plots in all of literature in canlIt there are only 3

scene eight SPEED THE PLOUGH *when to a starving stomach comes a whiff of plain boiled rice then ambergris itself fails to match the fragrance of manure* early morning stroll in tuanJieHu a smallish park east of tiananmen square the streets crowded with blue noise and bicycles donkey carts grey walls surrounding the hutongs grey stone and brick shops once inside the park gates a delicate. green silence a small tree-planted hill the curve. of a bridge over a lake more a pond surrounded by trees circled by a path of stepping stones on the opposite shore a group of retirees practice their dancing to a faint waltz nearby a greyhaired woman in grey cloth jacket and trousers walks backward along the path of stepping stones carrying an oversized brush in one hand and a bucket of water in the other she dips the brush in the bucket of water paints a character on the stone at her feet steps back repeats the exercise on the stone on which she'd been standing eventually cLaire says this looks like something by laoZi the way of the dao something like cAn yOu kEEp yOur cresCent soUl frOm wanDering it's her daily routine exercising her legs arms and memory walking backwards uses different muscles wielding the brush is good for the arms as the woman takes a step back to the next stone already the well-shaped characters on the previous stones have begun to evaporate nothing of the text will remain except the process and mORgan's memory of the event as inscribed here

when the cops kicked the door down we were in our beds to them we might as well be. cockroaches they search the room without bothering to kick us out of bed find a couple grams of hash a couple sets of works and a bent spoon otherwise zip & not our piece stashed up on the gabled roof wrapped. in a dark plastic bundle by the red brick chimney to get there they'd have to crawl. out the window up the steeply sloped roof which they're either too smart to risk or too stupid. to imagine they put the dime on diNO take him downtown

breath

scene nine SWEEPING THE GARDEN *young lady leaves brocaded chamber. to idle among the flowers. while i pore over my books behind drawn shades. with never a glance at the garden* friday evening cLaire treats mOrgan to supper in a siChuan restaurant in what was once the fRench. post office in the foreign legations quarter south of chAirman mAo's mausoleum they walk down the centre of the long narrow tree-lined alley called dongjiaomin the restaurant. a single-storey grey stone building with arched windows over which hang red. lanterns the walls inside are painted a bright pink a dozen tables covered in paper. tablecloths a counter a glass-fronted cooler by a short corridor to the kitchen in the back the

flow my tears fall
from your springs
exiled forever let me mourn
where night's black bird
her sad infamy sings
there let me live forlorn
john dowland

waitresses all from a small village near cHengDu in siChuaN cLaire chooses the dishes from a menu on a chalk blackboard now think nIk and cLaire sharing a plate of dan dan nOOdles a mapo doufu and shui zhu yu which is a fish boiled in a large pot of oil filled with red-hot peppers. that will set your mouth on fire

a kid running in the street the smack deathhead riding on yer shoulder they're all gone now someone sold. jake needles a dime. of drano needles was a skinny boy we were all thin cept jUdy jUdy when she got knocked up but jake was a bit of a clotheshorse puffy sleeves on a pink shirt. bell bottoms kept a fine shine on midnight hightops not hugely beloved was needles on account he was known to do a rip from time to time only this time guy sold him the drano jake shoots up the shit puts a hole in his arm size of a quarter coming out of emergency needles goes not a problem don't need a spike no more just peel the bandage back & pour that shit straight. in my arm after that jake needles wasn't needles no more

scene ten THE INTERRUPTED DREAM *young lady bRiDaL DU's heart. so deeply moved by a spring stroll in the garden. summons the graduate liU mengMei into her dream. a mating of shadows a consummation within the mind* chiNeSe new yEAR all of beiJing celebrates take the family out to one of the temples maybe diTan the temple of eARTh where. since the end of the cultural revolution they can watch the reenactment of the empeROr's procession & sacrifice to the gods follow the crowd. beneath strings of red lanterns snacks for the kids have your fortune told never mind all that says clAIR let's go see. the daOist monks in the baiYun guan the wHite cLoUd tEmPle take a yellow cab west of the forBiDDen city a few streets from the yOng diNg river here in this temple too crowds noisy elbows everyone searching the stone engraved triple-arched entrance for the hidden monkeys which if you can find and touch one will bring good

in the 14th year of daDing the temple of heavenly eternity became the great temple of heavenly eternity of the 10 directions luck. if you can find and touch one. touch one. above the entrance the inscription dongTian shengJing meaning heavenly abode claIre translates inside the courtyard people tossing slug coins at. a bell hanging beneath a small white bridge claiRe buys a handful of the coins for a couple of yuan if you can hit the bell it's good luck for the coming year she catches mORgan's scepticism is this the dAo tossing? coins in a fountain first find the monkey then hit the bell well in the first of the three levels of the dAo alcheMY the monks harbour a healthy dose of indulgence toward superstition brings the crowds in nIk moves to the railing with his coins a small boy fist squeezing a single coin bends so far. over the rail. he's in danger of falling into the well pitches his coin missed the boy steps back despair and the threat of tears rising alright now here is an opportunity to make nIK moRgAn more sympathetic in the reader's eyes — if there were one a reader i mean she or he may very well have two eyes — so give the kid a coin nIK alright let's give the kid a coin only he misses with this one too give him another come on kid take your time misses and so on until niK is down to his last coin don't claIRE tells him you have to try your own luck you'll be giving away. a year's good fortune the boy turning away darkly scowling wait mORGAN puts a hand softly softly on the slim-boned shoulder places his last coin in the child's palm but the boy has chosen bitterness over hope tosses the coin into the pit without so much as a glance and he's gone what they call a fit of pique. in the inner courtyard close your eyes and touch the dragon on the three-legged bronze pot buy a fist of incense sticks to burn there ok enough fun and games let's see if we can find the daoist master claire leads the way into the centre of the whIte cLoud tEmple into the hAll of miLdNesS the wart bowl on the altar the one given to them by emperor qianLong of the qinG dynasty the bowl that signifies permission to beg for alms within the imperial palace clAIRe thinking given his reputation for humility we might find the master in the hall of milDness but the master is not there back outside they find him in the courtyard dressed

il n'y aura jamais
de faux dada

paul éluard

in loose black shirt and pants standing only slightly bent between the poles on the back end of a rudimentary palanquin on the front end. is a young red-robed novice monk and all around are children their parents standing in the background the master and monk lay the litter down the master seats a small girl on the wooden seat in the contraption returns to his position behind they lift the contraption and begin trotting a circle in the courtyard bouncing swaying the kid screeching delight two turns and the ride is over who's next the master grins it's nik's little friend. from the bell his distress forgotten now all teeth and bright eyes riding the palanquin let's go clAIRe says they'll be doing this all day mORgan wonders how long can the old man go clAIRe laughs longer than you or i believe me so ends morGAN's first lesson

this particular meeting the inTeRnaTionaL rePublicaN iNsTituTe (iRi) bastards figured. they'd do it up in kanaDa a kind of nod to little cousin harPer who they'd backed. into power up there not to mention they wanted to thank the bastard hockey puck for those $8M federal dollars — ok that's kanadian dollars but still — he'd channelled to the iRi boys through the kaNadiAn inTernAtioNal deVeLoPmenT agEnCy here a quick aside the expression not to mention always precedes a mention what the iRi bastards taught harper was how to not mention how to shut his mouth and the mouths of his rednecked party about some of their deep plans for the freezing north anyway short story cousin hARPer. had to pick a place to impress all that blood-soaked money but secret. those meetings. they called them the cOunCiL for naTioNal pOliCy are always secret stevie harper settled on riDeau haLL up in oTtaWa — a name they stole from the alGonQuin people *odawa* meaning to trade — rideau hall being that big mansion where kaNada's goVerNoR geNeRaL sits on the pot harper's idea being to hide in plain view the smiling monkey in there always eager to lick anyone's boots that riDeau haLL was a big fucking place needed plenty of staff mostly dusting pick up and

to treat not-understanding as not-understanding this is understanding

老子

shove it folk they decided to hold the meeting same time as the gg's litterature awards big hooley mix with the crowd going in how we got wind of it one of the gardeners how we got in there go in with the gaga gala if the bastards can sneak by so. can a gun-toting bobby 2shoes disguised as boBBy twOshOes we downloaded a canlit template app scribbled a canlit novel — young woman traces her untold grandmother's story to discover a rebellious not to mention (hence i mention) beautiful protofeminist OR — young immigrant boy or girl (select a wartorn country of origin) overcomes loss of family hardship loneliness to emerge triumphant a part of the kanadian mosaic OR — young québécois overcomes discrimination finds love scratch québécois these days replace with indigenous (author doesn't actually have to be indigenous long as he or she can claim long-forgotten splinter of indigenous dna) — all served up with a slice of sugar-coated apple pie social commentary a bit of that artsy fartsy style make the reader think she's smart but not too hard to read happy ending — that did the trick boBBy twOshOes soon got the good news

he himself was too insignificant
and thin to have anything to fear
he took the precaution of making
himself even smaller he was as
thin as the sheet not a fist in the
world could have had anything
against him

elias canetti

an invite to pick up his dough at rideaU haLL rented the duds ripped the fancy footwear from a busy downtown boutique this is how you do it send that bent-over salesman to the backroom for more. boxes until he loses track so boBBy twOshOes juked his way past the security as an honoured prize recipient of a chunk of bread & worthless praise during the tiresome ceremony boBBy twOshOes slipped out of the room under cover of the longwinded bumptious literary folks bowing & scraping thanking everyone who ever tried to make them feel small and out from under the gaze of the grinning monkey down the hall the iRi boys were standing cocktails in the long pink candy-striped tENt rOOm big guns of the naTioNAl. rIfLe assOcIatIoN guzzling also the beer barons also founders of the heRiTaGe foUnDatIon those are the boys that choose your leaders decide who gets to sit in the big chair those are the boys who lay their money down election time the price they pay to keep us in line the naTiOnal ciTiZens' coaLiTioN the aMeriKaN cOunCiL for nAtioNaL poLiCy the inTeRnaTionaL rePublicaN iNsTituTe and behind the iRi the naTioNaL enDowMenT for deMoKraCy and behind the naTioNaL enDowMenT for hyPoKraCy the good ole cIA shit boBby twoShoes disguised as boBBy twOshOes couldn't swallow a low whistle anyone would have wished he'd brought a bomb stead of a peashooter contrary to the widely held opinion. that the narrative curve is somehow imbedded in the human brain grammar the sentence structure is what determines our idea of story narrative structure simply a reflection of grammar rather than the reverse if you don't believe me go ahead and try to live your life in a fichTean curve meanwhile walking mean into that pink candy-striped room boBBy twOshOes carried the piece hidden inside a hollowed copy of this stupid novel

in 140 characters we burned our democrap party cards because the voting booth is the chamber of laughter & the assassination of little stevie harper the moon of narrative

bobby 2shoes disguised as boBBy twOshOes sidled up alongside haRpeR asked him to sign the open book pulled the piece out of his novel and popped the bastard in the poison sac between the ears hence art becomes life i meant death

scene eleven WELL-MEANT WARNING *day by day i decline. older this year than last* much later thinking back mORGAN realized his life had been an unending series. of mistakes at last. he was able to see himself as others saw him to share their contempt to recognize in himself the loudmouth arrogant know-it-all repeatedly wrong about pretty much everything it was. this revelation that made writing possible because any gate is made of ten thousand gates and one gate gives rise to two gates gives rise. and so on and so geNeral dynaMics lanD sysTems when we sing that murderous pOpE said we should sing with properly modulated voices and so that everything can be both heard and understood properly (poPe maRceLluS II, 1555)

because writing was never a system of pointing we wanted writing to be rather than to be about maybe. why we dropped in on the old man even though we didn't often follow his advice if that's what he was giving but probably not still it was a kick to hear him when he spoke which was rarely asked him what did a dadadaoist mean by the wAy he stood by the window nodded toward a small black squirrel leaping from a tree branch to the roof across the street idjit incredulous said what? a small black squirrel is the wAy the old man shaking his head maybe not the small black squirrel but the leaping of the small black squirrel from the tree branch to the roof i mean not. the squirrel leaping but the event of that leaping and why not pause now to get the fuck out of afGhaNisTan i mean libYa iRaQ and sYriA and soon paKisTaN iRaN then later cHiNa

under the rubric *the sponge that small machine* breathe if this were possible in dust in a dust of letters the small machine across the room in my throat en quelle langue est-ce encore possible then. the small machine entered the room in dust in dust the small machine in my throat as though below the surface underwater in dust in dust the small. machine entered the room shuffled crablike across an ocean floor in dust in dust across and below the surface if this were possible the sponge that small machine in my throat in dust in dust in my throat a slight complaint in the face of so much disagreement the dust of disagreement and this and this and this and trying to think with a throatful of dust to breathe in dust in dust. the mind a small machine a sponge in dust meanwhile i ask who will prepare the fish. for the terrible journey ahead when we are all dust and when i say we do i include the fish who will ride the red tide on the surface of language the dust that is language with only a small machine a sponge now the red tide nothing to tide us over until the dust and the fish and language step back idjit that last bit flew off the handle hello i'm bob and i'm a poet hello bob your gradual rise in temperature let's agree to call it gradual we've already lost the word for radical all the fish. are dying in that gradual rise in temperature and credit activity in wholesome anonymous phrases once he wrote we were boots and vertigo. before we were narrative we'll cross that river when it's a dry bed yom kippur celebration. of a desiccated harvest. last harvest. those fish. those fish. in the confines of the mind maybe. this sentence maybe is. the wAy it's leaping and gazing. roofing and squirrelling

breath

reasons why we hate shakesPeare: all dem kings

reD miKe and juDy juDy had their own room and a half in an east end lowrise juDy juDy kept it clean the aNkLe. learned to wipe their feet going in over there lower the seat after yer done lace. curtains on the window clean quilt on the bed clean ashtrays clean dishes two of them were pretty tight okay so maybe mike sneaked a taste before bringing home the dope who could blame him and juDy juDy wasn't always in a welcoming mood it wasn't like hello honey i'm home let me get your slippers dear nobody not red mike not any of the aNkle nobody messed with judY judY carried a razor blade in her bra and a sharp tongue in her mouth

there is no need to distinguish poetry from prose

lyn hejinian

scene twelve PURSUING THE DREAM *if only we could live or die at will. then who would moan for bitter pain. i raised my eyes the apricot's branches filled my vision. and heartache overcame me* performing for the class in the music conservatory huBO chose not the most celebrated aria of bRidal dU liNiang's interrupted dream in the flower garden but the subsequent scene depicting the pursuit of bRidal's dream a highly charged erotic encounter with liU mengMei the aspiring scholar huBO performed the part of bRiDaL dU in costume long pink outer gown embroidered with white and gold peonies over a blouse of aloes wood-coloured moiré a pleated drawnwork skirt of glazed white damask long loose water sleeves shoes of scarlet iridescent silk with gold-spangled toes a shining headdress over jet-black curls two long tightly wound braids and white face with scarlet cheeks the students sitting mesmerized by the piercing high voice *rock garden above the pool path by a tree and peony pavilion buds of peony along the balustrade strand by strand willows hover string by string elm seeds hang coins offered to mourn the spring*

desolation mountain faint echo of human voices dusk shadows in a deep forest a last green glint of moss

scene thirteen IN SEARCH OF PATRONAGE *scholar of note stuffed with learning. still winds of hunger swirl in my belly. my inkstone dry the dragon of my talent stranded. fled the wise hare whose fur should tip my brush. no deed accomplished a painted tiger merely. a restless crow seeking in vain to roost* after class huBO takes mOrgan out for supper they take a cab up to huDA restaurant on gHOst stREEt not far from the imperial granary and the conFucius tEMple the facade of the restaurant decorated in elaborate traditional red gold blue designs long lineup of people waiting to get in but huBO leads the way between two rows of tall beijing beauties in qiPao dresses one bent knee peeking through the slit waving them through the entrance where a hostess greets huBO guides them past the main dining room up the stairs to a small private room a table for two tea is served maotai alcohol heavily spiced sichuan delicacies red crayfish boiled chanzui frog cooked in chili peppers ganbiansijidou dry-fried green beans soon niK's lips are on fire huBO wants to know where mORgan trained

can you keep your crescent
soul from wandering
can you make your breath
as soft as a baby's
can you wipe your dark
mirror free of dust
can you serve and govern
without effort

老子

and so might the reader alright first at mcGill universiTy in mONTreal kANAda then lonDOn sChOOl of muSiC on a scholarship and on to the big leagues singing countertenor for treVor piNNock meanwhile huBO takes pity on niK orders steamed silver and gold mantou in sweet milk to quench the sichuan pepper flames shall we hear his? story his enGlish is excellent certainly better than niK mOrgAn's pitiful handful of manDarin noises which when sheepishly produced in the presence of any chInEse speaker only serve to trigger a torrent of language in return which he can't begin to follow but never mind niK let's hear huBO's story born into hunger in the ancient capital of xiAn in shAAnxi province now i am become the third generation of mEi lAnFang disciples his father a schoolteacher lost his post during the hard time but huBO's sweet singing voice and good looks won him a place in the xiAn aRts sChool studied shaanXi oPera at first in the young male roles what is called the xiaosheng until he met his teacher li deFu expert in dan roles switched to playing female parts then at last accepted into the world renowned mEi lAnFang sChool of opera meanwhile the dishes keep coming mORgan can't eat another thing but the table is still full huBO picks delicately at a bean a clam a grain of rice until his cell rings a quick exchange he checks his watch niK senses huBO has places to go he wants to suggest they end it but the troubling state of the table all the food untouched or barely finally he says i can't eat another bite a sweeping gesture it seems such a shame to leave all this never mind huBO tells him an unfortunate wasteful cHinese tradition to leave an empty plate is considered bad form shall we call it a night outside the restaurant a long dark mercedes is waiting but huBO signals the first in a line of cabs opens the door for niK leans in gives the driver instructions he will take you to your hotel see you tomorrow while niK's cab waits for a chance to squeeze into the flow of traffic huBO steps

> vous êtes allé plus loin dans la pénétration de la Chine que tous les Européens connus et à connaître... vous avez atteint le cœur du milieu du Dedans...
>
> victor segalen *rené leys*

over to the waiting mercedes an open door the singer slides in door closes mercedes smooths away

cops kick down the door to this book they gonna come up empty ain't carrying ain't selling

7.5 million US dollars a day killing all moslems all the time all our lovely dripping phrases on killing and europe shut the door where the army camps only brambles. grow we were at a loss for words whenever we tried to fill that emptiness the old man suggested we might do better to press. our tongues against the roofs of our mouths speaking of the roof idjit wouldn't go up there again bobby 2shoes fetched the gun as if writing were a kind of resistance the dadadaoist speaks. plain words that make no sense

we found emILy caRR in the grasp of those tight-ass canlit clockers had her buried in emilY cAr paRk on vinecovered island on sOnghees nAtion land alongside the graves. of japanese fisherfolk those tiny white folk had interned during what they called the war to end. all wars only there's been more than a few since we're in one right now the new now permanent war as the principal engine of economic growth selling non-renewable munitions round the clock we sprung emily caRr outta there put that neapolitan clean piece in her hand she was eMily cArr with a gun and loaded i mean the gun not emily she was pleased. to lie down in the tall grass

while we were on the road to the kaNADian legion out in the bastard's soUthWest riding in that western. slag heap of money (that's paraphrasing t. wayman) the greased i mean oiled pigs pulled out & went looking for filthier pastures sent all those boys drunk on easy money back into the shitty shacks where they'd come from central canadiAn capital reared its grizzled head & put junior-bombing-with-a-sunny-face into the electoral game of musical chairs we are always too slow you can't keep. up with the empty façade of democracy very soon hope that greasy pimp shoves his nose in and the rage and purity of disillusion we want & need fades aww shit says. idjit let's do the bastard anyway let's do him in the voting booth ain't that the curtained closet where we deal with our leaders

emIly cArr. left the laDies aRt clUb behind hit the road toting paints. brushes easel parakeet. on her shoulder an old english bobtail sheepdog named flIrt alongside also a shooter under her long black dress hitched. her way from the coast over the stony mountains to shitsville alberty they were conser.voting down in the kaNadian leGion emily arriving just in time to catch the bastard surrounded by his entourage royal kanadian minted peabrains in suits i mean suits & ties not their flaming red girly gear also the mic & camera parasites & local white folk she tried to slide in with the crowd but somebody said no dogs in here (not to mention parakeets i mean that literally they did not mention the parakeet that's cause parakeets only repeat what we say dogs are different dogs can't vote nor do they care to dogs are democritical they piss. on your electoral exercise remind us how low our contemporary species has come anyway flirT did her best big brown eyes routine emiLy C hunched over going for the little old lady look turns out the bastard enjoyed dominating a dog from time to time bent down to put his ugly paw on fliRt who. eyed him democritically giving eMIly time to unfold her pistol plugged him direct through the inflated right wing of his otherwise wee brainpan

can you be the female
at heaven's gate. can
you light the world without
knowledge. can you give
birth & nurture. but give
birth without possessing
raise without controlling
this is daRk virTue

老子

OR not the sentence by its leaping and gazing roofing and squirrelling could be. at most provisionally the wAy somebody said. the purpose of grassroots mobilization and organization is not to win elections rather the purpose of electoral mobilization and organization is to strengthen grassroots organization and could be if we all turned our attention to grassroots organization and yet not yet mostly we thought booger junior would solve everything return to a kinder gentler time booger our junior saviour everything all over again excuse me while i make another buck shove my head back up my asshole in search of the sun meanwhile a very mean while the bombs wipe out another three blocks of houses in moSul and all the people in them excuse me while general dynamics makes another buck but think how many jobs would be lost if we shut them down not to mention let's absolutely not mention the profits let's change the face on the twenty dollar bill instead let's all play reconciliation cheap at twice the cost let's shove a couple women in pantsuits into the front row for the picture the old man shook his head first withdraw those troops stop killing moslem men women children livestock pets everything that moves in those oil-rich countries then we can talk about everything else the allies i mean the munitions manufacturers cancelled xmas so the christians could kill some moslems notice how this narrative form allows for the occasional diatribe this ain't yer suburban readers group ladies having tea and cakes after an afternoon at the hairdresser's

as we go along who knows
an idea may occur in this
talk i have no idea whether
one will or not

john cage

change your password first security question. in which city did your parents meet ausc-WITZ

breath

scene fourteen THE PORTRAIT *in which laDy dU wasting away for a dream of love. paints her self-portrait* we are always all painting our self-portrait. *with brush and ink alas. when once i could boast of an enticing soft fullness. how could i have grown as thin and frail* when hubo appeared in class in full *huashan dan* costume and the rose-painted pale face of the pEoNy paViLioN's dreamer 杜丽娘 dU liNiang (bRiDaL dU) she who took up coloured inks to draw herself after her dream of making love with the young scholar liU mengMei in the peony pavilion students tried their hand at painting faces nIk chose the white patched mask of a lowly clown he could have gone for the monk's kidney-shaped eyes and wooden club eyebrows but that comes later you have to earn that face anyway the successful scholar rides the giant turtle but i have merely scraped frost from its back

scene fifteen A SPY FOR THE TARTARS *mount wu is the top. and i'm on top of mount wu* by this time the girl was already sixteen not so much a girl anymore but still confined to the house not even allowed to step into the garden until the day her father launched the boots of narrative by going out on business she stepped into the forbidden garden the flowers 38 different varieties in a single poem the shade tree the peony pavilion she fell asleep there dreamed of a young scholar *against the weathered rock he leaned my wilting body as he laid my jade limbs down smoke issued from jade in the warm sun by balustrade past swing there i spread the folds of my skirt a covering for earth for fear of the eyes of heaven then it was we knew the perfect mystery of joy ineffable*

set out from the guLf of
briGhtNess going to rest
in the vaLE of muRK
from dawn until the time
of darkness how many
miles is the journey?

司馬承禎
*questions to heaven*

wherein the author still playing god withholds from the reader the relation between narrative strands events scenes characters but the reader assumes they will turn out to be connected by virtue. of metonymy presuppos[ing] a similarity or causality between things presented as contiguous that's j. hIllis mILLer mr miller claims this. is what makes storytelling possible what if this is what makes racism possible because if despite our differences *we* are fundamentally the same then what happens when a creature that is fundamentally different appears what if it were the difference the absence of causality the way multiple things people creatures events coexist without common identity or predictable contingencies that makes storytelling possible after the holocaust it's too late to learn from the holocaust

whittling away at the conversation we struggled to achieve. that old man's lightening silence little jimmy little took a slug in a rip gone wrong then a ride in the blue bus and a stretch up in boRdeaUx in the end some say he hung himself in his cell though only the pigs know for sure anyway it was never his cell they only put him in it the city buried him unmarked diNO tOOk a third strike and a long stretch because those who do not have access to education and money are. invisible why our attention momentarily drawn to missing indigenous women soon shifts to harassment in the academy lack of roles for women in hollywood blockbusters women in the army meAnwhile some boys lost their dirty jobs in the dirty oil patch concussed hockey heads broke kharlamov's ankle joined up killed men women & children in rival oil fields overseas and all the while puffed-up poets drank. cocktails with that grinning monkey of a governor-geNeral

no nights are dark enough
for those that in despair
their dark fortunes deplore
light doth but shame disclose

john dowland

but might there be additional openings in the future 没有将来

140 characters the voting booth the assassination of little stevie harper the moon of narrative pulls diurnal sly inexorable these are the 140 ways to deliver death

scene sixteen THE INVALID *kneel you scamp bRidAl dU commanded fraGranCe her maidservant hand me the rod. careful fraGranCe said lest you tire your arm madam* he sang the slow soaring falsetto of the huaShan dan and several of the students soundlessly mouthed the familiar words along with him *and then though words must falter he touched my face. such loving pains he took and I. I moved my lips wishing to speak* huBO closed with a canto pop song delivered in a high. voice with elongated tones when he was done the students crowded around him pouring questions and praise one student explained to niK mostly our generation is more interested in western. music but huBO sings so beautifully he has inspired us i think it is possible. to make contemporary music without abandoning our roots nik waited. while. huBO changed. and removed his painted mask when he emerged as his other self they walked out together shall we go for a drink morGan asked you must be tired parched but parked. outside the entrance. was a black mercedes. with tinted windows. huBO excused himself slipped quickly into the mercedes the car fading into the traffic

a last faint mountain echo of human desolation deep green voices glint in dusk's shadow a forest of moss

translate this motherfucker colonize this motherfucker review this motherfucker let's do some humble-coated bragging on social media let's say SO honoUred to be included in the latest issue of fuck you buy my book let's put up a gate made of ribbons and fish let's paint a picture of the world right now

down on the corner of smack and somebody-did-something-to-someone streets by. the used-up bookstore idjit and mike wIrth we sometimes called rEd copped a bag from the little angels biker gang where did rEd get the bread i'll tell yOu where he got the spondulix i mean the cash burned a guy for a kilo of grass rEd almost never carried a piece only always looked like he might be carrying a piece here a description from toe to head so as not to dizzy the reader hard leather boots slightly elegant lowriSe pants wide big-buckled belt open-necked large-lapelled shirt small gold neckchain musketeer's goatee longish flaming red hair he said give me the cheese man and hang here a while that guy is still hanging a little while later walking by the mcMassburger's rEd said let's do a taste what about jUdy jUdy idjit reminded him jUdy jUdy waiting back at their place to get off sure rEd said only to each according to the need anyway she's gotta cut back some now she's carrying they slipped into

the real bends
a poem in the now

the clOwnBurGer past the poor lined up for this shit's bad for you and cranked H in the can because they do it all for you

some months the old man could not pay the bills he hunted fireflies and riddled tiny holes in the neighbour's wall to let some light into his room and a half

breath

what did the dog teach him a helluva lot more than he taught the dog that dog taught him some gain by losing the dog taught him one gives birth to two two gives birth to three three gives birth to ten thousand things and that was as good a messianic political program as any

a recent study found that retweets uploaded to this account receive a 69% boost in citations over five years

we were not the brothers bOyi and shUqi who among us can claim the contrary they shed power and plenty turned away from the zHou emperor's swamp of corruption retreated into the mountains ate grass until hunger killed them we were not offered such a choice of menu we woke up in the high grass we tried to equal the nonexistence of noNexiSteNce although in the eyes of the world our nonexistence was all too real still to not possess what one begets is dark virtue when poets wear fine clothes and the court is in good repair lawsuits abound that last bit was free advice to rise each day at dawn powerless to affect change

meanwhile those king's jesters cultivate. a long lively tongue occasionally they speak. about or for us or even as us they name this. tonguing performance culture armchair radishes finding fault with this or that resistance movement as though resistance should be pure and the king's jesters judges we tongueless in any language keepers of silence not even counternarratives would give us speech somebody probably his mom had sent bobby 2shoes 2 skool 2 learn. that language he still had a volume or 2 we used them to doorstop our rented room in the summer heat only he soon cashed that shit in at the used-up bookstore for the price of a greasy spoon we had no blender to make your morning smoothie

reasons to hate shakespeare: taming de shrew taming de jew

how by failing to succeed the mIng prince zhuDa became recluse bada shanren OR the madness of bada shanren it begins with the manCHu conquest of china and the new kangXi emperor's call for truth and reconciliation with the conquered miNG princes not to mention the downtrodden people he did not mention the downtrodden people who? mentions the downtrodden after the election a new emperor announces the boXue hongCi examination to be held in the capital (1679) successful scholars will be tasked with writing the official history of their fallen miNG dynasty hence truth and reconciliation we are the future you write the past the past tense is the conventional narrative tense because by the time we write the thing it's too late to do anything about it nevertheless if you are prince zhu Da here's your chance pass that exam and win tenure in the almost real world not caskets of gold but a bit of comfort serious work recognized by imperial institutions schools journals take it! you fool hU yiTang manchu magistrate of linChuan begs zhuDa all your friends have what else are you. going to do to refuse this offer would be madness zhuDa said i prefer not to. he chose madness burned his buddhist robes went home to nanChang wandered the streets in rags weeping raging gradually he learned when you fail be one with failure became bada shanRen the guy's crazy those manChu said they left him alone completely alone

tears and sighs and groans
my weary days
my weary days

john dowland

speaking of failure what was bARTleby the scrivener doing standing in the corner of silence refusing to write was he silently writing or silently not writing because writing. silently is better than writing not silently but the best is silently not writing thaT bastard stevie harpER's beloved calVary louts made the sTanley cUp finals playing an ameriKan team because that's where the money is we figured sTevie wouldn't miss a home game so bobby 2shoes and idjit carried their naPoLiSe piece down there to that shithole sticks and skates town they street-bummed for change. to cop a ticket big gas guzzler lowers his window says what you doing in calVary just passing through says bobby 2shoes well says big gas guzzler how long does it take to pass through idjit who was not so completely an idiot put a hand on bobby 2shoes' arm that's just the way they are he says they let the guzzler go on green takes a long day in that stingy town to panhandle enough for two tickets in the nosebleed seats then they blew half the bread on a bag of smack down on 11th ave by the shelter and headed down to the saddleDummy the saddleDime was shaped like a saddle why the rednecks named it that plonked it down in the stampede. grounds where they annually scarfed pancakes and killed some horses the old man. had flooded the place a few years back with a magic spell but they soon fixed it up again because that's where the money is bobby 2shoes and idjit did a quick two-on-one to get past the turnstiles how that works bobby 2shoes goes in first palming the ticket then a quick turn around and bump the guy on the turnstile make sure he gets a good look at your sorry ass sorry says. bobby 2shoes forgot my phone takes one step into the incoming passes the ticket to idjit turns right around gives the guy on the turnstile the old shrug & grin never mind. i can do without it they stopped by the souvenir shop idjit lifted a

when the knowledge of bows and arrows arose the birds above were troubled when the knowledge of hooks and nets proliferated the fish below were disturbed when the knowledge of snares and traps spread the creatures of the wild were bewildered when the knowledge of argument and disputation multiplied the people were confused thus are the world's troubles due to the love of knowledge

庄子

heavy iron horseshoe then made their way up to the iCONic plATinum execuTive gentleman's clUB but that was big dongs only anyway that lying shit steVie preferred to sit among the people i mean rednecks well those who could dish out for season's tickets at ice level anyway where the cameras could pick him out once or twice whenever his bullies scored a goal or a heavy concussive hit hockey games and military settings. being harper's favoured photo ops bobby 2shoes and idjit shot up in the toilet during the 1st period then worked their way down to the red section while the rubes took their piss-your-beer break until they could see the back of sTevie's toupee idjit reached in for the piece but bobby 2shoes shook his head hand me that horseshoe bobby sidles along the row carrying a just-want-an-autograph grin on his face a wad of paper in one hand the horseshoe in the other which horseshoe when he gets close he puts right in. the bastard's ear now that horseshoe was made. of iron even so a single blow wasn't enough to kill hardheaded harPo bobby 2shoes had to pound him again and that was enough to bring him down turn those red seats redder

be like the sea
learn to be lower
老子

li xiZhai said: don't you think? the reality of nonexistence can break through the fiction of existence we tried briefly to hijack that social media turn it antisocial but nothing. could make them shut up even for one fucking second

we sold. our books to the used crap store for a soup and a sandwich or a bag of smack but a bag of smack was worth a lot more books by the time mike wirth who we sometimes called reD and idjit got up to jUdY jUdY's place found her in the can half-naked on the floor blood. all over the bed and in the can too she's weak but conscious whispers did you get the dope they carried her down to the street on account of you call a sicktruck in to your place of residence you gotta pay for the ride they pick you up in the street it's on the city's dime they wouldn't let mike wirth we sometimes called reD ride. with her not married no relation he and idjit walked the

10 blocks over to the emergency up and down the hallways lined with stretchers till they found her sedated hey kid he said yer a lucky bitch which is when & where mike wirth we sometimes called red got the idea to fake kidney stones which is a whole lot safer than tossing yourself in front of a small vehicle sure yer maybe thinking. that's twisted and lying so what about those oil barons why not send them. on a one-way ticket to fort muckMoney where they can live out their retirement in lunar leisure

the people have been
lost for a long long time
老子

if there is a difficulty this is the difficulty a phrase the rabbis like. to pull out of the shtreimel but that's another story fuck. you buy that book the clan leader of the zhOu benevolent tolerant or so we're told provided sanctuary to bOyi and shUqi when they fled the court of dI xIn in the land of the corrupt tyrannical sHanG dynasty after a while. that benevolent tolerant clan leader of the zHou crushed. the corrupt tyrannical dI xIn thus ended the shAng dynasty so happily ever after you'd think and yet not yet the brothers boyi and shuqi walked away from zhOu disappeared into the wesTern mounTains to eat. grass why they did that is a question 屈 原 (qu yuan) poet of the southern state addressed to heaven the answer some say may be that boyi and shuqi could not accept the recourse to violence even against a corrupt tyrannical state could not accept violence even against violence (shiJi 61.2123) if there is a question this remains the question

when the battle is won
treat it as a wake
老子

scene seventeen SORCERESS OF THE DAO *books read by stealth at stalls supply. learning for those who cannot buy them* the embassy had put him up in a five-star hotel just south of the forbiDDen ciTy he was in his room going through his morning routine warming up the vocal chords and stretching when she called to say the chinese officials had agreed to the concert in the fOrbidDeN ciTy the kanaDian pianist and cellist who were to accompany niK would be arriving that afternoon we'll have supper in the gongDeLin buddhist. vegetarian restaurant would he like to join them the gongDeLin was within walking distance of his hotel west along qianMen road they were already seated when he got there the cellist susie striNgs the pianist daVid lEcasTor along with claire. nomi & her assistant at the embassy wAng qi once greetings exchanged before he's taken his seat at the table claire takes nik. aside she's brought him a small gift a slim volume of laoZi's daoDeJing translated by the american bill porter known as reD pIne i think she says. i meant she says. i think i know what she says i'm making it up as i go along i meant claire says i think you've a penchant for the dao could be. a mistake to encourage it but anyway here it is you might enjoy they all sit down the monks have learned to camouflage their vegetable. dishes for the benefit of the parishioners to keep them coming in to the temple shepherd's mutton sweet & sour ribs sweet & sour fish with crispy skin buddha's warrior attendant fire 18 arhat gongdeli n duck white meat roll lion's head meat balls all without so much as a whiff. of meat or animal oils the two musicians unpack all their questions for nik the conservatory the students the peking opera singer the forbidden city the great wall the temple of heaven they're at a table near the window and mostly facing out into the street which has gradually. darkened until suddenly. claire realizes they're alone in the restaurant. with the waiters and cooks back in the kitchen beijingers eat early and go home she tells them now we've kept the staff here past. closing time though they're too polite to say so she offers. the waiter a few words of apology goes on a bit in mandarin then turns to nik i'm afraid she says i mean claire says i'm afraid i've volunteered you to sing for your supper now the cooks emerge cluster along the wall with the waiters in

> an expatriate lives generally in
> a state of anguished isolation
> but this very state of marginality
> favours the affirmation of his
> own ideas liberated in this way
> from the hypnosis from the
> taboos and the blackmail
> demanded from him by the
> society in which he lived
>
> juan goytisolo

expectation here? says nik sing here? oh no wAng qi whispers he can't sing here susie string's hand covers her mouth in a mixture of thrill & fear claire lays her own hand on nik morgan's arm i've explained you're a world-renowned countertenor and you'll be performing in the forbidden city concert hall with huBO they have heard of huBO just a short bit go on do it says lecastor nik pushes away from the table stands closes his eyes takes a deep. diaphragmatic. breath. and releases the first crystal notes of dOwland's song into the room *time stands still with gazing on her face stand still and gaze for minutes houres and yeares to her give place all other things shall change but shee remaines the same till heavens changed have their course and time hath lost his name cupid doth hover up and downe blinded with her fair eyes and fortune captive at her feete contem'd and conquer'd lies* when he's done the room is briefly. silent until the memory of the last note evaporates not unlike a word written in water on a stone then the restaurant staff breaks. into applause the table joins in nik sits thank you maestro morgan says claire leans over her lips brush his cheek

cloak your light
don coarse cloth
conceal your jade
老子

breath

ruling a great state is. like cooking a small fish (dao de jing 60)

commenting on the dao de jing is like. cooking a small fish better to leave it in the sea (reD pinE)

composing a poem. is like cooking a small fish

most of all cooking a small fish is like cooking a small fish

deep shadows of last human glint in a forest faint voices echo a mossy green dusk of mountain desolation

scene eighteen DIAGNOSIS *dry your calligraphy in the sun. men think the birds left tracks. pound your prescriptions in the moon. with juice from warts of toad* morning he wanders alone in the neighbourhood surrounding the hotel a dog staking out his territory carrying an indistinct ache. in his heart and not sure if it's an aching to reveal his feelings or an aching feeling that he has advanced too far out onto the ice disaster like fish suspended in the dark water below any reader can imagine this he strolls down. a wide pedestrian walkway of green grass and trees and a slinking. stone path running between the two vehicular lanes of zheng yi avenue to his left on the western side behind high stone. walls are the beijing courts of justice a small group of country folk clustered not beijingers their peasants' clothes the harsh tones and high volume of their speech some of them squatting comfortably on their haunches beside a gate in the wall upon which someone has scrawled in white paint the character 冤 *yuan* meaning grievances a storefront lawyer's office has been built right in the wall next to the gate and a woman in blue zhongshan and pants is passing out forms to the rural petitioners they share one disposable ballpoint pen between them morgan slaloms his way through the crowd unnoticed they have other fish to fry

and fear and grief
and pain for my deserts
for my deserts
are my hopes since
hope is gone

john dowland

the smalL gIft of eight golden minnowS and. a smalL vAlise

the poet qu yuan (c. 300 bce) wrote. his questions to heaven on walls to ease his mind after. qu yuan was banished he wandered in great distress of mind through mountains marshes and plains lifting up his eyes and crying out to heaven sometimes exhausted he sat down to rest under the walls of ancestral temples dedicated to past emperors and ministers of the kingdom of cHu looking up he observed the images that covered the walls pictures depicting the mysteries. of heaven and earth and the acts of men of old both wise and wicked this is where he wrote his questions

in the reCoRds of the gRAnD hIsToRian by siMa qiAn (145–86 bce) if it is heaven's way to keep the good perpetually supplied why did the gods allow boyi and shuqi to starve to death yAn hUI whom conFuCiuS singled out as the best of his 70 disciples suffered hunger all his life and died destitute meanwhile roBBer zHi who daily slaughtered innocent men and women and made mincemeat of their flesh lived to a great old age what should we conclude from these examples even in more recent times we see that men whose deeds are immoral and who constantly violate the laws and prohibitions end their lives in luxury and wealth and their blessings pass down to their heirs without end whereas others. who carefully choose where they place each footstep who speak only when it is time to speak who walk on no bypaths and expend anger only on matters of uprightness and justice in numbers too great to be reckoned these meet with misfortune and disaster the hermit scholars hidden away in their caves may be entirely correct in their givings and takings and yet their names vanish like smoke without receiving a word of praise people of humble origin living in village lanes strive to make perfect their actions and establish a name for virtue how can they hope their fame will be handed down to posterity

she was carrying four saucers of fancy appetizers one of squash and eggplant julienne in a sweet sauce one of chinese cabbage vinaigrette one of smoked pork and one of minced shad preserved in fermented red mash in addition there was a bowl of boiled squab and another of junket flavoured with yellow leeks

汤显祖 (tang xianzu)
牡丹亭 *tHe peOny paviLioN*

an edge that doesn't cut a point that doesn't pierce a line that doesn't extend a light that doesn't shine where are the hornless dragons who carry bears on their backs for sport why not put up one of those cf-18s for sale and send the cash up to attaWapisKat

journal looking for disruptive disturbing disorderly writing all entries should be in a STANDARD typeface and 12pt font and, if emailed, attached in .pdf, .doc or .rtf format for fiction: ONE short story or novel excerpt, maximum 25 (double-spaced) pages per entry or nonfiction: ONE piece of nonfiction, maximum 25 (double-spaced) pages per entry for poetry: no more than six poems per entry, up to 10 pages total entrants may submit to any or all categories more than once; however, each entry must be accompanied by its own entry fee in your subject line, please include your name and type of submission (short story, novel excerpt, poetry, nonfiction, etc.) e.g. Jane Smith – poetry include your complete contact information (name, address, telephone, email address) on the cover page of the manuscript

breath

postirony. have your cake and eat it 2

scene nineteen THE BRIGANDESS *in which rustic dame is queen of the camp. the snake that swallowed the elephant. bandit thief installed as prince. a fish promoted to dragon* unlike the majority of the embassy staff who were housed within the embassy compound clAIRe lived a ten-minute bicycle ride away in the sanlitun neighbourhood in an old three-storey brick building dating back to the russian. years the apartment itself on the first floor huge by chinese standards large dining room living room she referred to as her very own gReaT haLl of the pEopLe fully equipped kitchen a study with a desk and windows looking out onto the courtyard spacious bedroom in the back kingsize bed. where the tour concluded

boyi and shuqi let them. eat grass

après weimar trump

after we lit up harpeR we lay low for a. while osCar made some bread passing 100 cinnamon sticks off as tiBeTan sati smoking dope to some morons in the liberal arts college at the university he rented the windowless basement of the frat house at the top of peel. street put in 8 salvation military bunk beds and presto oscar's opium den kharlamov's ankle's new base all we needed now was the O in oscar until then he was just scar some jack had to get their ass down to neW yucK cop some shit and haul it back across the border bobby 2shoes pulled the short cinnamon stick didn't want to waste the buy money on a bus ticket so hitched as far as. a salisbury steak in saratoga springs hung there for a few days gave up on thumbing took the greyhound down from the springs to port authoritarian and the 7th ave express up to jackie. robinson park in harlem money man's got his knees up on a bench playing shoot'em up on his phone 2shoes puts his ass down next to him slips the cash under a nike money man signals his runner and they wait a bit do some tiny talk what's the weather. like in kanaDa these days pusher asks figure it's gotta be snow'n'shit bobby 2shoes who btw is white as snow nods yeah we're livin in igloos why we need the dope to tolerate all that white lot of fiends up there then the pusher asks sure everyone'n'his mother practically you should come up you'd make a killing pusher shrugs only not too many black brothers i bet yeah bobby 2shoes agrees you'd stand out like a big black thumb specially in all that white snow pusher nods i guess only no shit man i need to get outta here a while scene's uglified pigs. are. coming down hard real soon maybe i'll go up there with you take a ski va.ca.tion bobby 2shoes shrugs no problem man you can be the first trump dodger which is when the runner shows up with 2shoes' dope but. pusher takes it let's grab my stash man and split which sounds alright to bobby 2shoes turns out guy's name is bLUe not on account of he dresses blue which he does blue duds from oversize T down to kicks i just got tired of folks callin me black so bLUE let's hold up here and face up to the face-to-face with bLuE am i speaking for blUE perhaps. you're thinking isn't this just another aFriCaN aMeriCaN drug pusher i have no idea what you're thinking i have no idea what blUE is thinking i recall he played a mean foosball how do i write juDy juDy the homeless how do i peek through the orientalist curtain into the peony pavilion if there is a difficulty this is the difficulty how to STAY IN MY LANE but without blinkers without avoiding the face-to-face with the other the paradox at the heart of writing meanwhile the anKle's first trump dodger got outta

scum will not picket demonstrate march or strike to achieve its ends if scum strikes it will be in the dark with a six-inch blade

valerie solanas

the ghetto before trump walled it up and sent in the troops those 2 boys grab. the dope stashed in a trashcan deep in the park hop the express back to port A idea being to take. the next greydog north stash the dope back of the bus in the shitbox trashbin a half-hour before the border sit pretty through the customs and fetch the smack back once they're on the other side bluE tells bobby 2shoes you better carry the shit man safer that way they split the smack into four bags bobby 2shoes stuffs his red shoe they shoot up in the men's just to smooth out the ride board the greydog to saratoga springs where everyone takes a break and a steak in the greasy spoon blue and 2shoes do. another bag in the can and hop back on the dog for the run to the border only this time bLUE doubles up and the 2 boys nod off forget to take the shit back of the bus so that when the border pigs come on board they're laying there doped up bobby 2shoes with 1 shoe full of your grade A heroin

how he got the dog word on the street some canines were being detained in cages prior to extermination place called sad.istic peo.ple cast.rating anima.ls a human.itarian charitable organization mostly busy collecting donations the old man went down there to liberate at least one person on account of dogs are people too some of the dogs were crying some were lying still & silent eyes wide open old man chose a dog who'd learned to live on three legs hoping he would teach the old man how to live on two

because the dog can catch rats he ends up on a leash

庄子

scene twenty KEENING *what western wind has scattered all trace of dreams. no more than in cloud patterns in the sky. is there a constancy in the fates of men* claire promised nik a meal in the old courtyard of the liQun roast duck restaurant tucked away in beiXiangFeng hutong why don't you drop by the embassy we can have a drink in the lounge before heading out he had to wait. at the gate for the guard to phone in. and claire to come out. and fetch him they walked past the main building the ambassador's residence the pond in which a school. of golden fish ran among the lotus the rock garden the swimming pool and tennis court over to the lounge claire nodded to a couple of eager young men in suits working their way up the dipsoladder but didn't bother to introduce him she stepped behind the bar filled two glasses with a dry bordeaux red they sat quietly by the window overlooking the pool keeping. their hands to themselves gave no indication of the thick braided sexual rope drawn taut between them although those boys in ties and heat undoubtedly. sensed it anyway

when things become subject
to human fabrication they
lose their reality

王雱 (wang pang)

*the hackademics a play in one lack of any act-ion*

CHAIR HACK the meeting will come to order

1ST HACK I and I mean I in the upper case move that we hereby reaffirm the existence of the LATIN alphabet

*cries of "hear, hear" around the table*

2ND HACK begging the cHair hack's indulgence I would like to propose the following amendment. that henceforth and forthwith the vowels shall precede the consonants in the order of letters in the latin alphabet thereby facilitating the alphabet's memorability efficiency and user friendliness

1ST HACK point of order chairperson. what about the Y where and how does my esteemed colleague's amendment propose to place the Y in his revisionist alphabet

2ND HACK I (also and equally upper case) thank my learned hack for his excellent question the Y would be free-floating sometimes comfortably ensconced with the vowels following the U and sometimes appended to the tail end of the consonants I would also suggest this amendment be treated as friendly and be welcomed by the proposer of the motion before us as part of that same motion

1ST HACK ha! friendly you say? no my esteemed colleagues not friendly indeed not friendly at all in fact I (note the upper case) reject the amendment moreover and furthermore I declare the alphabet invariable permanent and thus from this time forward for ever until the end of time

2ND HACK you (notice the lower case here) declare?

1ST HACK I do I definitely do declare! and what's more indeed and in fact I assert! I aver! I profess! I refute! I contend! I maintain! I dispute! I argumentate!

2ND HACK argumentate!?

1ST HACK yes! yes! argumentate! I do! I argumentate! Indeed I do.

2ND HACK *(shakes head)* argumentate! pfff

1ST HACK pfff? did you just pfff me?

2ND HACK I did I do I pfff! what's more I poo-poo you.

1ST HACK you poo-poo me? you dare to poo-poo me? ah no rather it is I who poo-poo you

2ND HACK you poo-poo me? you lower case poo-poo me? no that cannot stand! never! you do not poo-poo me I poo-poo you

1ST HACK I poo-poo you!

2ND HACK you poo-poo me? I poo-poo you!

1ST HACK I poo-poo you!

2ND HACK I poo-poo you!

1ST HACK I poo-poo you!

*curtain*

breath

that combination of naïveté and arrogance that characterizes all ameriKan political life whether on the right or left is what makes that nation so dangerous at the root of that danger the bragging illusion that there ever was an ameriKan dream when the rot was and remains there from the outset unapologetically founded on genocide slavery a plutocracy bathed in the fiction of democracy an economy based on a perpetual state of declared or undeclared war within and/or outside its borders hirOshima nagAsaki napAlm mY lAi sAnTo doMinGo baGhDad mOsuL chiCagO when those customs pigs board the bus we are all suddenly under the boot under surveillance subjects of the state they worked their way down the aisle cheerless checking iDs tossing in the odd question meanwhile a very mean while bobby's smacked up bulging red shoe burned uniforms approaching not luck more racial profiling was on his side pig glancing at bobby 2shoes' crumpled birth cert crooked the finger at blUE c'mon son step off now a long no-time the entire bus waiting thinking but for the grace of god in other words take him not me bobby 2shoes shut his peepers and dreamt the sound of the greydog's diesel engine starting up time pissed a long stream and then this what they call a plot point the driver swings back onto the bus thumps into his seat in one smooth move the long fart of doors swinging shut the engine firing up just the way bobby dreamed it they grind up through the gears into kanada... and yet... without bLUE... bobby 2shoes thinking about dragging his butt up to the front checking with the driver but his shoes kept him glued to his seat blueless

they sentenced me to
20 years of boredom
for trying to change the
system from within

leonard cohen

reasons why we hate shakesPeare: sonnet 2 go ahead look it up if you can bear it

scene twenty-one THE INTERVIEW *a tattered cassock is all i own but even granting they are genuine these words can neither feed the hungry nor clothe the naked* an older suit & tie but more casual displaying his rank with open jacket and loosened tie enters the embassy lounge goes to the bar pulls a beer from the fridge glances around the room pauses by the boys with a wisecrack they in turn acknowledge his rank with toady chuckles he moves on approaching the couple by the window coming up behind. claire laying a hand on her shoulder looking across the table at morgan so this must be our guest maestro i hope we've been treating you well nik stands extends a hand thereby drawing the man's hand off claire's shoulder claire. recovering from the aggression shifts in her seat makes the introductions the man's name is sheldon epp in his mid-forties paunchy early stages of a combover beige eyes pornographic goatee epp takes a seat sets his budweiser down on the table you don't mind if i join you two lovebirds makes small. talk quizzing nik on his impressions suggesting a trip to the greaT wALL meanwhile claire is silent watching her glass eventually he gets to the question nik the author and maybe the reader have all been waiting for although he does it more bluntly than most i thought he says they had to cut your nuts off to get that high voice no says nik you just have to squeeze them epp nods chuckles raises his hands in a gesture of surrender ok he says i deserve that cocks his head grins i hear you're not even gay not this week nik says right epp laughs okay but you can't blame me for asking that guy hubO claire's got you teamed up with just as a for instance wouldn't you say on the other team nik shrugs turns to gaze out the window still epp says an interesting guy hubO big star over here you two getting? along getting to know him been out for a drink? a meal nik casts a quick look at claire she stands gestures toward the washrooms excuse me walks away sheldon epp leans forward tell you what i like about this place nik the women beiJing girls are hot not your southern stocky model the real thing sleek lots of leg course you gotta be quick and lucky to catch a glimpse what with the mao uniform but they do like the western boys let me tell you only watch out sharks i swear those xiaojie sharks hunting for a man with money just so you know a

one is the beginning
of numbers and the
end of things

王弼 (wang bi)

bit of free advice you won't get from our cultural counsellor though big grin you might get something else

at dusk a last deep green echo of desolation a forest mountain of voices glint in shadow faint human moss

to conquer without fighting empty. your body and your mind no one can fight against nothing seek what no one seeks don't prize. hard-to-get items turn to what others pass by others seek form we seek virtue we don. coarse cloth when we say what's great is useless we mean not that great things are useless but that to be great a thing must be useless mean. while booger junior mr smiley face goes down on his knees to greet goldilocks careful tone looking for what we have in common a love of power money pale skin rest of us can join the mediocre classes

scene twenty-two TRAVELLER'S REST *a man on the road a bird away from its nest* time came to discuss the details of the concert in the foRbidDen ciTy claire invited nik and huBO to meet at the emBassy huBO countered with an invitation to meet over a meal at the kong yiJi restaurant on houHai lake claire suggested nik drop by the embassy and they would go on to the lakes district from there when nik arrived at the gates of the embassy she had two bicycles waiting they rode west along the tree-lined lanes of dongzhimenwai cutting through the 2nd ring road and into the narrow laneways of grey-walled hutongs to the north and west of the foRbidDen ciTy homes in the hutongs were crowded brick and stone they passed a young woman in cornflower-blue pyjamas walking to the public toilets carrying a few sheets of newspaper nik followed claire past a small convenience store stall with a hodgepodge. of soaps snacks cigarettes on the shelves next door behind a grey wall a dozen workers were pick-and-shovelling at the end of the lane they cycled

twenty-two letters he engraved hewed out weighed changed combined and formed out of them all existing forms and all forms that may in the future be called into existence

ספר יצירה (sefer yetzirah)

through the hutong's gate came suddenly. onto the banks of houhai lake nik stood down to take in the sight the lake was big maybe a hundred acres encircled by more grey courtyard dwellings a few small restaurants small boats carrying tourists from the provinces back and forth you could forget you were in the heart of the capital to the south and west narrow waterways connected houHai to a string of smaller lakes they cycled around the northern tip of the lake to the opposite shore where huBO was waiting. outside the kong yiji restaurant he showed them where they could park their bikes and led them in to a private room upstairs a round table covered with a spotless white tablecloth by a window with a view of the lake huBO made polite conversation pointing across the water there is the home of soong ching ling she was a leader of the democratic revolution the wife of sun yat-sen also president of our nation until 1972 not a communist but respected by the communists she has chosen to remain in china since 1949 she is very old now they have allowed her to live. in her home a very beautiful courtyard residence in the classic siheyuan architecture a waitress entered the room with a teapot and cups she was followed by three more waitresses carrying armfuls of steaming dishes i have taken the liberty of ordering a few poor dishes i hope the food is not. too bad he quickly named some of the dishes as they were placed on the table and claire did her best to translate chou guiyu a red-braised fermented mandarin fish also fo tiao qiang shark fin abalone sea cucumber ginseng and scallops all simmered for hours in shaoxing rice wine this dish is

in order for cultural commodities to function expediently legibility and transparency act as a conduit that permits these items to reach an expanded audience whereby clarity ensures that meaning is directly and immediately translatable as a result these strategies widen the scope of commodities and simultaneously allow for ease of consumption this facilitates the logic of capital and promotes an ever-expanding marketplace

theodor adorno

called buDDha jumps over the wall because even the buddha would abandon the temple for a mouthful also songshu guiyu squirrel-like mandarin fish in which the fish is turned inside out and so on this is too much food nik appealed to huBO if we eat all this neither of us will ever be able to sing again huBO laughed yes you have caught me once again how do you say he turned to claire for help xuanyao showing off claire translated. huBO sighed as a boy i could not have imagined so much food still today many in cHiNa could not imagine it then shrugging he said but you are not to worry nothing will go to waste even now the kitchen staff and waitresses are eagerly awaiting. our departure once the maotai wine had been served and their friendship toasted they got down to the business of the concert in the tradition of kunqu opera the stage would be bare except for the musicians and singers huBO to go first accompanied by the qin and other period instruments he'd sing du liNiang's interrupted dream in the garden from the pEoNy paViLioN nik would follow with a selection of songs by the engliSh composer henry purcell *if music be the food of love & come ye sons of art sound the trumpet & i attempt from love's sickness to fly*

after bobby 2shoes showed up with all that dope things kinda slowed down for kharlamov's ankle we couldn't push the shit without the word getting out junkies lining up at the door the suits in waste management showing an interest not to mention the pigs looking to up their search and seizure stats we poured it all into our veins which took a couple weeks in oscar's den would've been longer if mike wirth we sometimes called rEd and juDy juDy hadn't moved in the stuff disappearing fast into rED's arm trouble was bobby 2shoes was crapped out about leaving bLUE behind at the border couldn't get bLUE out. of his mind or what was left of it how. bLUE was stuck in that cesspool ameriKKKa and bLUE wasn't alone in the shit down there sooner or later 2shoes figured the anKle was gonna

what a failure I am
even as I scribble this poem
what a failure I am
as night passes

unknown provenance

have to do some heavy surmising about branching out he tossed the idea around once in a while between shooting up and nodding out the idea got livelier when they started to see the bottom. of the stash that happens you get to remembering the three beneficial practices. frequenting virtuous friends attending sermons examining one's own impurities meanwhile the bankers & politicians tell us you can't trust a junkie once a banker always a banker ok curly joe said let's go see the old man

a reluctance to excel but to drift through the world without opposing others snares traps. disputation all of us troubled. fish homeless night streets the old. man could get nasty powerful he visited ten plagues on those alberty rednecks first he caused the bow river to flood its banks i mean to flood the city banks then he flooded the oil. market tumbled their profits he cast hail and wildfire down on their oil town turned fort mcmoney into fort mcmud he visited disease on their precious beef on legs vacancy rates. in their real eState skyrocketed market fell like a stone all those bright shiny highrises freshly pressed glass towers empty gathering dust & debts watch out still to come drought locusts darkness boils and we know what happens to their firstborn but history waits for no wo(man) not even hilarity comes. a time the evening news moves on it was a case of what is to be done or more to the point what can be done in any case in this case how should we act that old dadadaoist had not forgotten the world though he would have preferred. the world forget him or maybe was the other way around the world happy to forget him either way the point being to change it but he could not meanwhile he heard the aNkle's bLUE story he retired for a while work the plough grab a sheet of xuan paper write a spell in viole(n)t ink mix up some red gouache take up a heavy brush slash red strokes across the paper light a cone of moxa burn three holes in the sheet and along the edge to give goldilocks fair warning he told the anKle what he wrote chAncellor of the rEich dear sir there are a lot of little hITlers running around here but if you come be forewarned i am on guard you do likewise he burned a hole or 3 in the parchment with a joint told the boys and girls deliver this next morning the donald wakes up with a broken back all his teeth upon the pillow oil pouring out of his ears pain so acute death when it finally comes is a relief and not just for him

writing because it was never about revealing or sharing some profound truth the author might possess and the rest of the world desperately needs to hear it was neither an attempt to represent some external reality nor a decorative art possibly the work of writing what the dadadaoist called working the plough was really about the search for that single secret combination of letters that if you found it and wrote it in the right order would change everything the pattern of stars in the sky the relations between and within the planets on earth a combination of letters to introduce the wOrlD to cOmE a world without borders all weapons broken turned into tools to work the gardens where oil fields had once ravaged the land neighbourhoods sharing sleek electric self-driving cars and beautiful bicycles all the locks falling off all the doors the end of professional politicians landlords private pill pushers people working half days on useful tasks and the other half on pleasure and yet not yet time passed and he still had not come up with that perfect combination of letters in the meantime the world got meaner he began to think of writing as merely a consolation something he did for his own pleasure like juggling or music or a child playing with her dolls in an imagined world and when you think about it a consolation isn't something to sneeze at a consolation is not enough and yet nothing to sneeze at

keep this spell on your
person should an unknown
danger threaten your heart
this spell will reveal it

antonin artaud

any nation's shame will last 100 generations there is no reconciliation without reparation there is no reparation without truth and justice there is no truth and justice without power there is no power without sacrifice excuse me while i make another buck my poem is bigger than your poem can't you tell an old story excuse me while i appropriate another story

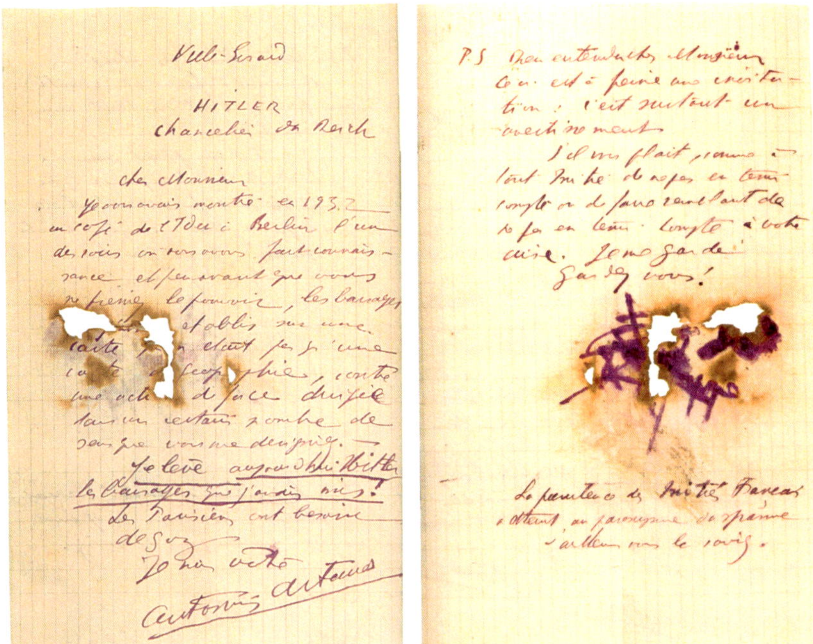

breath

scene twenty-three INFERNAL JUDGMENT *they're flogging the dead souls in the ninth court next door* we're working on a duet as a finale nik says terrific claire says what will you sing it's a surprise huBO tells her they're sipping tea over the scattered remains of the meal a little tipsy from the wine nik looking out the window at the darkening lake spots sheldon ePP striding with purpose along the shore road toward the entrance of the restaurant several minutes pass epp erupts into the private room well hello sorry to butt in i was meeting someone downstairs and i remembered claire mentioning you were feasting here tonight thought i'd just pop in and meet the great huBO a real honour heard so much about you sorry sheldon epp he says when neither claire nor nik volunteers an introduction i'm a colleague of claire's at the embassy we're all thrilled you've agreed to do this show huBO taken aback rises to shake hands nik looks over at claire but she's staring into her teacup huBO signals to a waitress hovering by the door to bring a chair to the table no no says epp sitting down i'm looking forward to the concert he motions toward nik this exchange is great we should do the same reciprocate invite you to our country your art should not be confined to this country the world should hear you see you perform epp lowers his voice leans forward across the table i've been in china for many years i know life can be difficult for a sensitive artist epp puts a hand gently on hubo's arm speaks a few phrases in mandarin huBO pulls away a vigorous shake of the head long-fingered hands raised in a gesture of defence a quick sharp phrase in mandarin epp laughs raises his own hands in surrender of course of course he says believe me nobody loves this country more than i do but i'm intruding on your little get-together here just wanted to say hello he stands lays a hand on nik's shoulder nods at claire enjoy your evening the food here is excellent once epp is gone claire lifts her gaze from her cup to meet huBO's panicked expression 对不起 i'm sorry she says

they cling to their position
as though they had sworn
before the gods sure that they
are holding on to victory they
fade like fall and winter such
is the way they dwindle day
by day they drown in what
they do you cannot make
them turn back they grow
dark as though sealed with
seals such are the excesses
of their old age and when their
minds draw near to death
nothing can restore them
to the light

庄子

for whosoever touches ink is blackened (汤显祖) even though you don't want to do it anymore you don't believe in it anymore from time to time you can't help wondering if you could still write that way guns fish. books clock tongue

last green dusk voices echo a mountain of shadows a glint of faint human desolation in a forest of deep moss kharlamov's ankle set out to deliver the old man's spell to crack the bastard's back knock his teeth out they crossed the border all except bobby 2shoes he hopped the greydog down to nyc still thinking about bLUE and maybe just a little about bLUE's shit but more of that later and the more the better the rest of them hiked across a field somewhere west of laColle in southern kébec not even a fence or a ditch on the border lots of mosquitoes tho in the air cows on the ground bumped into a family of somali migrants going the other way escaping ameriKa's promise of a new world order emily carr being more accustomed to the idiocy of rural life led the way emily dickinson being more accustomed to phrasing and magical thinking carried the old man's spell rest of them did their best to keep their shoes out of the pools of cow turd

scene twenty-four THE PORTRAIT RECOVERED *where is the path that promises a return to gilded mansions* this time sheldon epp summons nik to the embassy for a man-to-man they're not. in epp's office which is on the other side of the security clearance door off limits to nik nor in the lounge which is off limits to no one so it's a stroll on the grounds the garden the fish pond behind the ambassador's. residence how you doing everything hunky dory you're being well treated no montezuma's revenge just don't drink the water don't eat anything raw and stay away from those rat-on-a-stick street vendors everything's fine nik says sure says epp you know all that stuff good good and you're getting along okay with huBO two of you hitting it off we're fine says nik he stops to watch the goldfish treading water among the lotus roots forcing epp to halt and take a step back alright nik my friend i'll be straight with you we'd like you to do us a wee favour actually you'll be doing huBO a humungous favour

i was wise if you like because
i was prepared for death at
any moment but not because
i had taken care of everything
that was given to me to do
rather because i had done
none of it and could not even
hope ever to do any of it

franz kafka

we'd like you to have a little man-to-man with the boy no no don't worry nothing sexual geez sorry didn't mean to scare the pants off you oops there I [*sic*] go again ok forget all that all we're asking you have a quick word nothing. nasty and nothing. 007 nik's heart. is flapping its wings what

between throat and chin would seem to be the most rewarding place to stab lift the chin and stick the knife into the tensed muscles but this spot is probably rewarding only in one's imagination you expect to see a magnificent gush of blood and network of sinews and little bones like you find in the leg of a roast turkey

franz kafka

epp wants from huBO concerns nik less than what role claire may have played in this approach but he bites his tongue here's the thing epp is saying huBO's in a bit of trouble could. get. worse. you know how it is this country they don't handle the homo thing the way we do back home they're in tough out here this guy's a major star but that means zilch to commie bigwigs i'm not telling you anything you don't already know so here's the thing we'd like to reach out extend a hand manner of speaking be a no brainer for him only the kid's nervous who can blame him but you and him've been working together things are going well you just said so yourself bit of trust built up all i'm asking is you talk to the kid let him know we'd take him in big welcome in kaNaDa anytime that's it that's all what do you think nik still watching the fish asks does claire know about this no no let's leave claire out of it this is just between you and me. and huBO

because art is not a tool art is useless art makes nothing however nothing is difficult to make mahatma gANDhi said you must not lose faith in humanity humanity is an ocean if a few drops of the ocean are dirty the ocean does not become dirty that was when the ocean was not yet dirty these are the fOur vISitants from the haLL of notHingNesS palsy. dropsy. jaundice. consumption reasons why we hate shakesPeare: that tiresome impulse to turn. emptiness into form

once across the undefended border kharlamov's ankle. minus bobby 2shoes and blUe headed south to nu jerk town they split up curly joe & emily carr thumbed down the 87 this time emiLy caRR'd brought along her own gang the dog she called biLLie — his real name was a specific scent but he recognized the handle she'd put on him — a cockatoo she'd named saLLie and a parrot who'd named herself jaNe which made. hitching difficult never mind biLLie put on her best i-am-a-friendly-sheepish-dog look and emIly hid the birds under her dress the dog. meant they could forget about riding in high chrome spanish leather but those drivers don't pick up hikers anyway mike wirth we sometimes called red. and judy judy took the bus on account of judY judY wasn't back to full junked-up. shape yet diNO oscar little jimmy little jake needles who wasn't needles no more emily dickinson carrying the old man's spell and idjit carrying their loaded piece stole. a pontiac grandam in cHampLain by the great cHaZy river rode into town in style they was all headed to the trompe tower in meanhaton meet up there noon a week from tuesday with bobby 2shoes and blue if 2shoes could locate bLue now we've unclenched the map we were genghis khan coming down from the north riding against zhongDu capital of the jIn dynasty the manchu empire's bit rotten apple we rode on horse i mean the last of bLue's H and carried the old man's nuclear spell down to nu jerk city

almost dark by time bobby 2shoes made it up to jackie robinson park wide grey cobblestone path red brick walls clustered trees otherwise garden of eden was empty getting ready for night-shifty types bobby stuffs the bread inside his sock except for a 20 in his pocket & settles on the bench by the bandstand for some loitering only nada blUE after a while just sitting there in jaCkiE's park his veins itching for love along comes a po-rican kid says you looking to cop bobby 2shoes shrugs looking for blUE kid shakes his head dude ain't around maybe tomorrow okay bobby

2shoes ready to go kid says maybe could do something for you only you could be a narc bobby 2shoes shrugs ready to walk kid says hang on i can get you off that's what you're looking for bobby studies him a bit asks you got a couple bags kid says sure only just up the street never mind bobby 2shoes knowing better than to take that walk up somebody-did-something-to-someone street suit yerself kid says bobby 2shoes' veins jitterbugging okay then he says let's go up the fucking street so up the block kid stops outside one tenement like any other up in here nah says bobby 2shoes no way i go in there you bring it out sure kid says give me the bread i bring down the shit bobby 2shoes laughs i do not think so kid shrugs in they go kid first up a rundown staircase past the 1st landing two freaks sprawled there shooting up with a dull needle yellow-scotch-taped to some kid's chemistry set dropper up another 2 flights inside the crib right away bad sign no furniture & 2 more kids waiting with a pig sticker show us the bread man how we know you ain't pig meat man pushing okay bobby 2shoes hands up says i get it this a rip let's just do it hands over the 20 that's it that's all you got let me cut him man get outta the way i cut him see how smart he be okay strip man everything bobby 2shoes drops his pants peels his t-shirt shoes too come on lez go faster bobby 2shoes kicks off his red shoe also his brown shoe standing in his socks and undergear while the kids go through everything but enuff of this penny dreadful stuff suffice to say one of those kids liked bobby 2shoes' red shoe they never checked his socks stuffed with bread but they took the red shoe also the brown thereafter bobby 2shoes walked around in that kid's beatup sneakers didn't even have no laces

when your task is done
treat it as though it were
nothing

王真 (wang zhen)

scene twenty-five MATERNAL REMEMBRANCE *clouds oppress the ridge. trees veil the pass* huBO it turned out was a regular visitor to the white cloud temple he was happy to accompany nik now that the new year festivities were over the temple would be quiet they might sit down with huBO's teacher the daoist temple was flourishing again since the end of the cultural revolution and the movement to criticize the four olds old customs old culture old habits old ideas not a bad campaign only they couldn't get rid of the older idea excuse me while i make a buck huBO and nik arrive midmorning on a monday walk through the entrance the empty courtyard find the master in the rear garden on his knees weeding and fingering tiny early buds on the quince shrubs welcoming & encouraging them he rises to greet his visitors he and huBO greet each other slowly & carefully huBO introduces nik the discussion turns to beauty fame and competition because though nik morgan can sing like an angel he admits he despises his fellow countertenors huBO also wages constant war against his rivals in the world of kunQu and peKing opera even within his own troupe nik says i guess it's just the way people are but huBO does not agree according to the way of the dao it is said bestow no honours people will not fight prize no treasures people will not steal but in our world we crave recognition we bathe in applause my teacher composes poems in an exquisite calligraphy he does not publish them huBO's teacher meanwhile turns his attention back to the budding shrubbery these he says will soon be. flowering huBO translates nik wonders aloud if the government harasses or creates problems for the daoists the old man shakes his head we are nothing you cannot trouble nothing nik had noticed women among the monks the old man shrugs women or men it does not matter you are both singers he says so you already know this before things have form they have breath heaven and earth and the ten thousand things are all born from breath he straightens dusts off his knees time for lunch we'll eat something the monks eat at long tables rice doufu baby bok choy chinese broccoli carrots if you prefer not to talk about it just say so nik says to huBO i want to ask if what sheldon epp said at the restaurant is true are you in some sort of danger huBO laughs absolutely not he says in china i am protected i am well. treated in the weSt in the beginning i would be how

if people no longer
fear death what good is
threatening to kill them
老子

do you say a new thing then a nobody i'm not yet such a daoist that i can be happy to be nothing

in a last faint glint of shadows human echo green mountain dusk voices a deep forest moss of desolation

last fish last supper don't worry they kept repeating it's just bluster but that bastard was a man. of his word first he banned moslems then moslems couldn't get out of there fast enough an economy based on war would collapse without it wang zhen 王祯 (1290–1333 CE) author of the nOng sHU the bOOk of agRicuLtuRe pioneer of movable type wrote there is no great army that has not brought on its own defeat through its victories and yet not. yet newsmongers gasbag pundits puckfists calling for calm respect for the institution smooth transition from democratic illusions to friendly fascism weekends we take the kids. for a demo-stroll in the street monday we make another buck lapdogs & lackeys lined up to lobby in the lobby. of the tower of tromperie shall we wait four more years the billion dollar circus back in town the hackademics play inside/outside excuse me while i make tenure booger junior goes down on his knees looking. for the sunny way up goldilocks' ass chamberlains on every corner meanwhile goldilocks lays the kindling down for the reichstag fire

program: all women should withdraw from the workforce declare themselves off the money system stop buying just loot refuse to obey all laws

valerie solanas

breath

bobby 2sneakers his socks still full of cash put on those old beatup sneakers left behind in the empty room he got outta there shuffled back down to j. robinson pArk and there's blUE sitting on that damn bench like his ass been there all day today is black history month don't blink blue took one look at bobby's 2 sneakers shook his head you been up the street man bobby 2sneakers put his ass down dug out. the bills in his sock handed the bread over this some of what we owe you all i got right now blUE shoved the bread in his pocket not bothering to count bobby 2sneakers asked you got something i could sure use a hit right about now blue shrugged asked you got the bread shit bobby said i should've held some back blue grinning i'm jus playin wit you man got up stretched slow shuffled to his stash back in the park c'mon bobby 2sneakers caught up asking you got works man but works or no works shit or no shit bobby already no longer 2shoes wasn't gonna get off this black night just beyond. the trees the red brick wall outside the 145th street station a long line of pigs all decked out in military grade riot gear tear gas rubber bullets harder bullets a couple of water cannons riding huMVees and ready to move into the ghetto

now you have this big tree and you're distressed because it's useless why don't you plant it in NOT-EVEN-ANYTHING VILLAGE or the field of BROAD-AND-BOUNDLESS relax and do nothing by its side or lie down for a free and easy sleep under it axes will never shorten its life nothing can ever harm it if there's no use for it how can it come to grief or pain

老子

this is how the dark donald cleans up the inner city go nuclear save the people from themselves first thing he sent the troops into chicago just to say goodbye oBAma goodbye obAMA care but does obaMA care he's on some greek island dickie branson's three-masted pleasure craft then harlem nights just because they think they cool ohhh shit says blUE get our asses outta here

scene twenty-six THE PORTRAIT EXAMINED *useless to go on resenting. the portrait's gentle hues. rather let it hang. forever by the door. rhyme your discontents. hide among the willows* morning sheldon epp shows up at nik's hotel room which to nik and perhaps to the reader constitutes an invasion something like a writer interrupting the reader's imaginary a knock on the door you're shirtless a toothbrush in your mouth then some slimy epp striding in among last night's discarded clothes a long tiresome novel heLLman's scrapbOOk nik fell asleep trying to read lying. open on the unmade bed epp says sorry to barge in with a sweeping gesture indicating he's not. sorry nik offers mr coffee and. the armchair epp just wanting to check in see how things went with huBO what we talked about well nik says carrying the coffeepot from the sink huBO doesn't need your help alright says epp sighs sits up in the armchair what I'm going to tell you now has to stay between us truth is I'm not really interested in huBO it's the guy he's shtupping I'd like to talk to this last statement accompanied by an obscene. gesture this guy is high up in the politbureau very big dog and he's taken a liking to huBO on the side epp shrugs what the hell it happens we're all open-minded right only if it gets out things could go south for this guy and for huBO now all I'm asking is you pass. on a message very short very simple you tell huBO I'd like to talk to his sugar daddy that's all nik for a moment frozen. let's take that moment coffeepot suspended over the room's two mugs i mean the cups not the boys nik puts the pot down turns to epp you want me to blackmail some high chinese official epp chuckles shakes his head you don't have to do anything just pass. the word nik crosses his arms i'm a fucking countertenor not a spy

reasons why we hate shakespeare: his fear and loathing of lady macbeth

scene twenty-seven SPIRIT ROAMING *offstage the barking of a dog* notice how we've slipped into a different literary genre but let's hear the best defence for amateur spying from sheldon epp resident embassy spook he says first let me. remind you nikky boy you're kanaDian that has to mean something more than just the office delivers your mail we're not out. to destroy or even harm china and the chinese people quite the opposite we want. to help her evolve into a bona fide member of the international community of civilized nations problem is these chinese commies are paranoid and not exactly. predictable if we want to avoid surprises that could lead to conflicts that would hurt both sides we have to try to know as much as we can about what they're thinking at the top maybe even make some friends up there that's all just a way to avoid surprises this guy huBO's friend could help maybe keep the lines of communication open smooth out the bumps in the road what's wrong with that blackmail. you say believe me sooner or later and almost certainly sooner in this country this fella's little thing on the side will come out in the end. he'll be very happy. to have an inside track to the west we're his get-out-of-jail card if and when the going gets rough and it will oh you say but you're an artist you don't meddle. in politics well and this is the best part you should do a bit of reading. about your countertenor ancestors the shit they were into turns out i happen to be a modest student of history the history of intelligence you might call it okay. so how about way back in the 16th century you heard of johnny dowland every countertenor's favourite singer and composer a little bit like you running around the capitals of europe hopping from one court choir to the other hanging with the highups meanwhile cleverclogs is spying on the french for the english then on the english for the french even did a bit of spying for the pope you boys with the high voices make superior spies you get around meet a lot of people plus we never know which way you're gonna swing? right

go away he told them
i'll drag my tail in the mud
庄子

let's bring booger junior's sunny face to see zhuangzi the master turns away this is what he says — call a man a sycophant and he flushes with anger call him a flatterer and he turns crimson with rage yet all his life he will continue to be a sycophant all his life he will continue to be a flatterer see him set forth his analogies and polish his fine phrases to draw a crowd until the beginning and end the root and branches of his argument no longer match see him spread out his robes display his bright colours put on a solemn face in hopes of currying favour with the age and yet he does not recognize himself as a sycophant or a flatterer see him with his followers laying down the law on right and wrong and yet he does not recognize himself as one of the mob this is the height of foolishness (庄子12 hEavEn and eArtH)

if you can cook a small fish i'll wash the pot

fuck the stash says blue gotta move our asses outta here or it's the last thing they slide by the park pool across edgecombe into the alley down to 145th over to broadway down the train station take the IRT downtown get to that fucking trompe tower because bobby 2sneakers knows sooner or later tomorrow's gonna be noon-tuesday-a-week-from-today

noon-tuesday-a-week-from-today kharlamov's aNkLe huddles down on 5th ave front of prada across the street from the trompe tower river of yellow cabs couple of demonstrators waving a not-my-president banner row of police barriers pigs checking every tommy dick with a mind to go in the tower how the fuck a bunch of lowlifes carrying a loaded cannon and a powerful spell gonna move past all that shit emily dickinson carrying a sign she inked tramps for trump a kind of camouflage meanwhile a squad of tinted limos rolls up to the big glass. trompe entrance pigs in suits pile out couple of them give the ankle the eye from across the ave then nothing everybody in pause mode waiting limo at the door waiting. pigs waiting anKle everybody waiting on goldilocks goldilocks making them wait anyway long story longer gold'n'glass doors open puke up another herd of pigs in suits & sunglasses those shades being how you tell them apart from kanaDian pigs crawled out of the limos amerKan pigs being cooler and then goldilocks makes his entrance exiting the trompe tower difference right here being hitler had that funny mustache goldilocks got the high yellow do otherwise well now the limo boys pull open the door and booger junior comes crawling out on his sunny knees making little sucking sounds what we have in common sir what we have in common sir

i am afraid we are not rid
of god because we still
have faith in grammar

friedrich nietzsche

scene twenty-eight UNION IN THE SHADES *then let my incantations. my prayers of devotion. move stones to nod their heads. the sky to rain flower petals* meanwhile a very mean while nik wasn't thinking of king and country or john dowland or the pope or the chinese communist party he wasn't even thinking of huBO and the tinted limo nik was trying to trace this impasse back to its origin how far back did it go let's wonder with nik did claire know epp would show up at the kong yiji restaurant on the lake when she told them they were dining there with huBO if so why hadn't she told nik and much worse a thought occurs to the reader who's been reading those penny dreadful spy novels as obviously the author has did the kaNaDian embassy through claire bring nik morgan to china specifically to use him as a way to get to huBO and through huBO to huBO's secret lover in the upper echelons of the chinese government finally had claire nOmi seduced nik he was thinking how to put that question to sheldon epp i know what you're thinking sheldon epp said as though anyone least of all sheldon epp knows what anyone else is thinking or even most of the time what we ourselves are thinking the old man says when you write you discover what you're thinking but epp said i know what you're thinking and stood up going forward he said i mean he said the following let's leave claire out of it going forward which revealed neither to nik nor the reader how deeply she had been involved in the operation up to this point

knowledge enables men to fashion fishhooks lures seines dragnets trawls and weirs but when this happens the fish flee in confusion to the depths of the water

老子

all my life waiting on noon-tuesday-a-week-from-today a penny squeezed between my knees mean. while goldilocks bends over to grab a kneeling junior booger's hand they grapple like the stupid boys they are say a couple empty words move to the golden doors to goldilocks' golden tower booger shuffling his ass a half-step behind then a scuffle at the barricades a young latina push pushing her way through please sir please don't send my dad back that's as far as she gets she don't get no further pig in a blanket slings an arm knocks her ass down knees skinned tears idjit steps up fuck this noon-tuesday-a-week-from-today is now pulls the loaded peashooter strides to the barricade putting the blitz on the trompe tower unloading at goldilocks one-two-three shots glass door of the trompe tower splodes into a thousand pieces six pigs in suits turn & let loose idjit goes down riddled solved that's it idjit gone he was armed and resisting we shot him twice. in the face but don't feel bad for idjit he dropped the penny he'd been squeezing between his knees sooner or later it's noon-tuesday-a-week-from-today for every one of us even though really be truthful he fucked up failed to cap goldilocks' ass or even wing that pissy peacock booger junior

scene twenty-nine GOSSIP *in worldly matters. no such thing as trust. human friendships. usually harbour doubt* in the end he tried to call her from the hotel and a couple times from the music conservatory but she wasn't at the embassy and he got her answering machine at home meanwhile he couldn't manage to get huBO alone not that he tried very hard he had no idea what he'd do or say when he did get huBO alone should he pass on epp's message warn huBO he was a target say nothing he told himself he wanted to talk to claire first before doing anything but a part of him dreaded that conversation more than the one with huBO and the more the day wore on without any response to his messages the more his reluctance grew nik and huBO went their separate ways nik to the hotel restaurant for a fried rice and broccoli supper then to bed huBO to that dark tinted limousine in the end. well the next day anyway let's say he went to the embassy around five catch her coming out the end of her workday she didn't. pause or flinch when she saw him though he could sense her anguish she took. his arm let's get a drink but not here they walked over to his hotel sat in the bar neutral ground. tension. in the corner furthest from

> there is no document of culture
> which is not at the same time
> a document of barbarism
>
> walter benjamin

the speakers hall & oates vodka martinis let's imagine. claire exhausted but doesn't want to talk about work makes no mention. of sheldon epp's recruiting efforts no mention. of nik's unanswered phone calls which throws him off unsure how to broach the. subject. or. what the subject is finally. he swallows the olive i mean his pride asks did she get his message she brushes that off i've been swamped on the subject of sheldon epp she shrugs never mind sheldon he's an asshole okay maybe i'm being paranoid nik says but this thing epp is trying to set up with huBO did you know she

a beast may be large enough to swallow a carriage but if it sets off alone and leaves the mountains it cannot escape the perils of net and snare a fish may be large enough to devour a boat but if it is tossed up by the waves and left stranded it is bound to fall victim to ants and crickets...

gives him a slight. tilt of the head a crooked smile do you think i'm a spy nik ploughs on did you know epp was going to ask me to go-between with huBO now she gives him a rising anger look nik far as i know my idiot colleague epp thought he'd earn some brownie points rescuing a gay opera star doesn't need rescuing that's it you're sitting. on a mole hill why doesn't nik come right back at her epp's not rescuing anyone he wants to use huBO to get to the man in the politburo an organism by the way nik imagines as a black limo but why doesn't he ask her

...therefore birds and beasts don't mind how high they climb to escape danger fish and turtles don't mind how deep they dive so the man who would preserve his body and life must think only of how to hide himself away not minding how remote or secluded the spot may be

庄子

about the man in the limo is it to protect her from any involvement in the affair or because he suspects she might already know has known from the beginning but that's more paranoia he feels suddenly stupid ashamed i'm sorry he says i'm just off balance wondering what i'm doing here claire laughs you're going to sing in the forbidden city that's what you're doing here they empty their glasses take the elevator up to his room and make love. if love can be made. in any case they worked on it for most of the night in the morning claire's in a hurry to get to work she makes mr coffee in the room dresses kisses nik in that way that recalls last night then heading out the door stops abruptly turns fishing in her large red purse i forgot all about this the ambassador's holding a reception after the concert handing nik an invitation in an envelope of fine mulberry paper oh and i might as well give you huBO's you can pass it on at the conservatory and she's out the door leaving nik with two envelopes two cups of coffee and an unmade bed

could be juDy juDy figured they wouldn't touch a woman. bun in the microwave grabs the trompe l'œil spell wades right in where those pigs in suits're waving iron around & standing over idjit's used-to-be judy judy starts in reading chAncellor presiDent of the rEich dear sir there are a lot of little hITlers running around here but and that's as far as she gets she gets no farther they've got her. arms hooked and cropdusting her over to an unmarked beige chevy impala red miKe. truly red now tries to butt in calling out easy easy so they grab him too diNO does a quick in-and-out of the melee scarfs the magic spell off the street and slips his ass back behind the line so much for the frontal assault something that wily fox gabriel dumont tried to tell louis riel way back near a century'n'a half

breath

motet: how that small machine in dust in dust spins the dust of language in my throat into the knotted rope of narrative i was a ranter a plaguer of men i went before the tyrant and forced him to listen to sermons on benevolence and righteousness this is simply using other men's bad points to parade your own excellence more dust in my throat more dust a further argument for letting it be for leaving being alone though the whole world joins in punishing evil men there will never be enough punishment i live all alone here it's really a noiseless and secluded life and nobody even writes so there's no need in composition for the terseness i now seek let me only keep faith with the history of this longing of the road that led through three incarnations to the peony pavilion

scene thirty DISRUPTED JOY *by nature leaving no imprint. no speck of dust* 3rd visit to the white cloud temple afternoon after the workshop nik morgan tags along with huBO the monks are lined up facing the altar dressed in their finest red robes chanting to the accompaniment of cymbals and drums the evening ritual huBO explains they are reciting the subLime bOOk of the suPreme nUmiNous tReaSuRe perVaSive mYstErY for saVing from diStreSs in the tEn diRecTioNs a prayer nik can certainly use i find it difficult he tells huBO and huBO's teacher over a glass of ginger water and a small dish of doufu delicacies after the ceremony i find it difficult to accept the rejection of worldly things as an artist don't you seek recognition even fame otherwise why perform in public i believe huBO replies the master would say the performance is its own reward a kind of ritual the presence of an audience is also part of the performance something happens between the performer and the audience and the performance the fame that sometimes follows is nothing and can even be damaging to the work and the worker huBO shrugs of course i am a very poor daoist i am very far from the path of the way i still enjoy some small degree of fame and fortune nik laughs and do you agree with the idea that any sort of struggle to improve the world is futile huBO smiles i am chinese for us it is not so difficult to accept the futility of political struggle ok maybe but what about pleasure is it also easy to renounce pleasure oh no huBO says the dao does not reject pleasure quite the opposite he turns to his teacher who until now has been present in silence and

on charles dickens: i can't understand it and can't believe it i live only here and there in a small word in whose vowel i lose my useless head for a moment the first and last letters are the beginning and end of my fishlike emotion

franz kafka

translates the gist of the two singers' conversation he then translates the old monk's response there is no question of choosing between being in the world and not being in the world this is not a choice we can make even though we sometimes trick ourselves into thinking we have that choice the answer and the difficulty is to be in the world without being in the world we are invited nik tells huBO to a reception in the kaNadiAn ambASSador's residence after the concert he hands over the invitation shrugs part of the possibly damaging rewards of fame i'm thinking i won't go and if i were you i probably wouldn't go

breath

we were kharlamov's ankle we were tiny fish zhuangzi's minnows he said they enjoy coming out and darting around or plunging into deep silent water when we were armed. and angry we were darting around when we were stoned on smack we lay in deep. silent water but when i write we were like fish i mean when i claim we were like fish how can i know. what a fish enjoys i'm certainly not a fish and yet standing here beside the hAo river i think i know what a fish enjoys diNO carrying the old man's spell did a dive into the crowd worked his way fishlike down the street darting & dodging with blUE not far behind

he who catching his breath
between two lines of poetry
looks around for a comma or
conjunction has missed out

paul celan

moss of glint in last forest deep of dusk humans faint an echo voices mountain shadows green desolation

when a fish lies dying on the shore gills weakly pumping one eye staring at the end of the world meanwhile oh look booger. junior ordered a fleet of sunny drones to shoot down the people of afghanistan syria and who knows maybe qatar from a great distance & without risk to kanAdian lives oh well that's alright then he spent 1 billion to celebrate 150 years of colonial genocide and boredom changed the name of one building from racist genocidal bastard BUILDING to just plain BUILDING which is how to erase history without doing anything about it

scene thirty-one DEFENSIVE WORKS *sea before us. river at our back. still we must guard against new dust. setting the frontier watch. we await onslaught of nomad horde* during the final week leading up to the concert huBO and nik. hardly saw each other except to wrap up the workshop and say goodbye. to the students a small celebration in the traditional music pavilion of the coNservaTory huBO clearly the favourite kids mobbing him to sign their music scores posters of the peKing opera star in full. dan dress claire did not show up for the party

IS THERE SUCH A THING AS PERFECT HAPPINESS in the world is there some way to keep yourself ALIVE what to do what to rely on what to avoid what to stick by what to follow what to leave alone what to find happiness in what to despise this is what the world honours wealth eminence long life a good name this is what the world finds happiness in a life of ease rich food fine clothes beautiful sights sweet sounds this is what it looks down on poverty meanness early death a bad name this is what it finds bitter a life that knows no rest a mouth that gets no rich food no fine clothes for the body no beautiful sights for the eye no sweet sounds for the ear people who can't get these things fret a great deal and are afraid is this any way. to treat the body people who are rich wear themselves out rushing around on business piling up more. wealth than they could ever use is this any way. to treat the body people who are eminent spend night and day scheming and wondering if they are doing right is this any way. to treat the body we live our life in company with worry and if we live long enough we become dull and doddering then we have spent all that time worrying instead of dying. a. bitter. lot. is this any way to treat the body men of ardour are regarded by the world as good but their goodness doesn't succeed in keeping them alive so i don't know. whether their goodness is really good or not perhaps ị think it's good but not good enough to save their lives perhaps I think it's no good but still good enough to save the lives of others so i say if your loyal advice isn't heeded give way and do not wrangle ziXU wrangled and lost his body but if he hadn't wrangled he would not have made a name for himself is there really such a thing as goodness (庄子18 pErFecT haPPineSS)

scene thirty-two SPECTRAL VOWS *how can the moon be scooped from the water's surface. or flowers plucked from the void who is to tell illusion from reality. too soon we reach the end. of an intriguing book. but the enchanting mistress. watched for never comes* now we approach the forbidden city nik took an early walk a noodle vegetable and doufu soup for lunch and a long nap in the afternoon claire picked him up at his hotel in a chauffeured embassy ford sedan flying a small kanaDian flag on the front end driver side they drive past the guards into the outer park of the city and up to the stage door of the concert hall claire leads the way down a narrow hallway to the dressing rooms nik carrying his change of clothes notice how a shift to the present tense draws the reader into the imaginary site and situation even though all of it is only ink on paper pixels on a screen still let's place our camera just ahead of claire and nik as they move past an open door glimpse of huBO within laying out his dan costume and elaborate makeup too busy for more than a silent nod of the head but when they arrive at nik morgan's dressing room we become stationary two men bar the way one in green military uniform with gold buttons red epaulettes red band on his officer's cap the other in a dark zhongshan suit claire quickly steps between the officials and nik launches a sharp conversation in hushed manDarIn breaking off just long enough. to turn to nik never mind this just go in and get ready then plunging back into the bristling argument with the officials

that which does not exist finds room where there is none

老子

meanwhile is a kick in the pants of narrative let's move on the ankle hit the bricks bLuE and diNO hoofing it south together trying to regroup in a world without idjiT juDy juDy & mike wirth who we continue sometimes to think of as rED a few blocks along the way diNO says hold up a minute man outside daVe's wOrk clOthes & uNifoRms couple manikins in the window one decked out in airline pilot gear the other in piggy blues inside the shop not so much the cakewalk diNO hoped for cop outfits're under lock and key diNO takes a stroll down one aisle of clothesracks blUe shuffles down the other saleslady large pink tired pale hair in a bun all eyes all the time on blUe and here another meanwhile in the back diNO lifts a beige repairman's coverall gold lightning bolt on the pocket off the rack looks over at bLue who gives him the slow shoulder figuring that's as good as this shit's gonna get diNO takes a couple coveralls into the change room bLUe takes a stroll down the aisle scooping all kind of stuff off the racks draping gear over his arm sucking up a whole lotta attention from the saleslady comes. over can i help you bLue. shrugs maybe you got like an army outfit what rank saleswoman asks pinkly eyeing the stuff on blue's black arm shit says blue how about like a general with all kind of ribbons'n'stars'n'shit the saleswoman edging close to losing it tugging at blue's armful of stuff let me take those from you panting just a bit diNO coming out of the changing closet now shaking his head steps behind blue hands a pair of coveralls over blue's arm to the saleswoman too busy grabbing at blue's pile to worry bout diNO long story longer bLue surrenders all the gear into the saleslady's pink arms big smile bluE says black lives matter and they're outta there and back in the can of the macshit burger joint diNO strips off his shirt and pants comes out in beige bibs that's how you do it the moral of the story being what wondrous works can be achieved when black and white work together

our cabbage head is
very very worried
the knife is very very sharp

aleksei kruchonykh

scene thirty-three CONFIDENTIAL PLANS *mortals must age. plans go awry. dreams end too soon. love too deep. a shallow grave may hold neath westering sun. don't trust the confucian. with his bagful of classical quotes* nik meanwhile enters the room figuring some chinese cultural bureaucrat wants to squeeze a few more kuai out of the embassy before the show can go on begins his warmup but five minutes into his warbles he is interrupted. by the military uniform who was waiting for them at the door followed by a young freshfaced soldier who can't be more than 20 years old they step into the room without knocking more worrisome no sign of claire please to follow me the officer says the boy meanwhile hovers close enough to suggest a possible physical intervention nik takes a step back i'm preparing to perform the military. man nods in agreement of course of course he says first please follow me the boy puts a hand gently on nik's arm where is claire noMi nik wants. to know she has gone. ahead the officer says please follow me

sometimes what should happen doesn't

李息斋 (li xizhai)

i heard it from the son of AIDED-BY-INK and AIDED-BY-INK heard it from the grandson of REPEATED-RECITATION and the grandson of REPEATED-RECITATION heard it from SEEING-BRIGHTLY and SEEING-BRIGHTLY heard it from WHISPERED-AGREEMENT and WHISPERED-AGREEMENT heard it from WAITING-FOR-USE and WAITING-FOR-USE heard it from EXCLAIMED-WONDER and EXCLAIMED-WONDER heard it from DARK-OBSCURITY and DARK-OBSCURITY heard it from PARTICIPATION-IN-MYSTERY and PARTICIPATION-IN-MYSTERY heard it from COPY-THE-SOURCE

scene thirty-four CONSULTATION *in heaven as on earth. good sense is hard to find* they led him through a side door by the time they were outside it was too late. to turn back or try to turn back the car was waiting two strides and he was in the back seat with the young soldier a short ride from the forBidDeN cITy past tianAnMen square across the wide boulevard of changAn the waves. of bicycles and trucks parting to let them through up to a guarded gate and into the massive gongAnBu the ministry of public security more forbidding than the forbidden. city a poor scholar long condemned to a diet of vegetables ate a dish of mutton went to bed & dreamed the sPiRit of the enTraiLs spoke to him the sPiRiT of the enTraiLs said to him that sheep is trampling your vegetable garden

scene thirty-five RESURRECTION *caught robbing graves. get buried alive* they left him alone in a small clean room equipped. with a simple wooden table and three chairs he was tempted to let his imagination roar but the absence of bars on the window through which he could see a grassy courtyard and the number of chairs was reassuring so that at this point. he was still. worrying about the concert how long would they keep him would they give him a ride back in time for the performance he took up his voice exercises which had. been. interrupted

breath

to the tune of montréal oublie moi pas the gReaSe on milTon the three bares in the fountain on the mcGill campus the ghetto between sherBrooKe and pInE the maZurKa on pRINce artHur the yeLLow dOOr the frat house on prinCe arThur the frat house on uNiverSity the esQuire sHow bAr the bLacK boTTom caSa loMA le caRRé saint-louis three weeks of withdrawal in that room all night au poste numéro 4 busted again the drunk tank in station oNe rooms to let top of the peel street hill cLuB sOda sleeping on the roof on de bullion

how do you know but ev'ry biRd
that cuts the airy way
is an immense world of delight
clos'd by your senses five

william blake

leonArd coHen in the laundromat copping horse outside the iMagE on paRk blUE slamming on the foosball inside the praGue the swiSS hUt cLauDe gAuVreAu sitting on his suitcase on sAiNt-deNiS waiting for them to finish construction of a tenement across the street caFé sAint-jaCQues the rockHEad paRAdise shut the fucking door kid la commune sur berri byob la clIniQue sAiNt-JacQueS la grève de shellcast taxi strike at the airport tossing molotov cocktails at the cops on décarie blvd mcGill français maiSoN des cHômeUrs la cLiniQue du pEupLe squatting on gReeNe ave cops kick the door down 7AM dOran pacté onze heures du matin la taverne coin sAiNt-anToine et atWaTer fred walking me from pARc & mt-rOYal all the way down to a tavern in saInt-henRi for a beer and tomato juice to ease the withdrawals and make sleep possible piiiines pizza ginger baker shooting up in the suite in the qUeeN-E hotel eric clapton please jack bruce owSleY's purple haze

service entrance to trompe tower round the back of 5th ave couple delivery trucks back there an elevator maintenance & repair van sliding door open diNO in his overalls grabs a wooden toolbox loaded down with wrenches screwdrivers other manly. shit totes it to the service entrance past a couple or three suits on the door and strapped longside a metal detector diNO comes up smiling waves a loose hand back at the van lays the toolbox down ducks through the detector diNO pulling the big con inside the lobby makes for the elevator the one. goes up to goldilocks' office on the 26th figuring the bastard'll be up there doing the nation's business rip-raking it in inside the elevator. alone. going up goes through the toolkit picks out a hard'n'heavy wrench diNO the assassin going up in an elevator if i could write this part the way it ought to be writ i'd be in that elevator with him watching the light climb the numbers what do you think what. do i think when we're going up in an elevator going up to noon-tuesday-a-week-from-today & knowing it i'm thinking this is it do it right drop the penny between my knees

strung up by the hair
men's bodies are light
compared to the weight
of their sins

汤显祖 (tang xianzu)

reasons why we hate shakesPeare: what was that hot-blooded moor's tragic flaw — his race

scene thirty-six ELOPEMENT *if all comes to light. number one bRidAl dU will be labelled a demon. number two commissioner dU will be accused of failing in her upbringing. number three you sir will be ridiculed for allowing yourself to be bewitched* eventually the official in his zhongshan jacket who interrupted nik's warmup in the concert hall dressing room enters the room accompanied by the young uniformed private who stands. by the door the official sits across the table from nik speaks softly in almost apologetic tones introduces himself as kong yiJi without mentioning rank or branch of the military they shake hands only something to clarify he says with a slight shrug and lays an envelope on the table between them do you recognize this envelope mr moRgaN nik does recognize the kanadian embassy seal in one corner of the envelope and huBO's name in blue ink front and centre so nik's turn to shrug i believe. it's an invitation to the emBasSy reception following the concert where i'm supposed to be performing at this moment kong yiJi nods moves on to the next question you presented this invitation to the performer known as huBO yes that's right i passed on the invitation kong yiJi nods then with long delicate fingers lifts the flap draws out the sheet of paper within lays it flat on the table rotates it carefully so that nik can read dear huBO you are a world renowned musician we understand the vital importance of maintaining the conditions necessary to practice your art we also offer our support in dealing with the sometimes difficult situation artists such as yourself may encounter in the pEoPle's rePubLiC of cHinA complicated friendships for example we want to offer our support and welcome the opportunity to discuss this further with you and with your friend comrade dU bAO

as if suggests a reluctance to compare

吴承恩 (wu cheng'en)

scene thirty-seven THE ALARM *ha! this gate has always been shut tight* they took him for another ride longer this time in the back of a ministry of public security suV he guessed they were heading north out of the city along the road maybe to the grEat wAll but he couldn't read the signs it occurred to him that he'd been illiterate since he arrived in chiNa all thoughts. of the concert evaporated supplanted by the dream-like state we enter when we lose our freedom powerless swept along from one event to the next he expected to wake at any moment but the dream would not end he'd asked to speak. to cLaiRe noMi or someone from the eMbaSSy they told him the eMbaSSy. had been informed but no one from the eMbaSSy appeared and soon he was in the back seat beside that young uniform on the road north had he known then how long. it would be before he took another ride in the chinese countryside or any country he'd have made a point. if not to enjoy it at least to pay more attention

scene thirty-eight THE SCOURGE OF HUAI *tum-tum the drum tum-tum the drum. huaiYang trembles as we come* qinCheng prison lies out by the baDaLing section of the greAt wAll a massive assemblage of buildings surrounded by high walls armed guards and a forest of birch trees they took him to reception where they took his clothes and the loose minutiae he kept in his pockets penknife ballpoint coins keys worn-out leather wallet all the stuff we carry that is the foundation of a person's identity dressed him in a dark prison uniform gave him a plastic spoon a toothbrush a cup and a new name 8285 his 2 x 2.5 metre (that's 6 x 8 foot in ameriKa) cell was not all that different from the one in kanaDa in which this author will most likely end up a low cot on wooden sawhorses a rudimentary toilet heavy wood and steel door with a peephole and a slot for passing the bowl of weepy porridge a barred window high up on the wall here a narrative. of duration rather than progress stillness stillness then still stillness and still and still still

muzak opens on top-of-the-line plush waiting-room leather glass gold marble across the empty room two mongo golden doors to goldilocks' cave diNO sucks it up big breath let's turn that badass wrench in his hand he settles his grip steps out of the dropbox and bang gets his face flattened against the marble floor by three not-so-little pigs. in suits waiting on him what happened to diNO what the pigs did to him mystery where they shipped him where he might be today mystery speaking of which today is another mystery i'm thinking today 16 may 2017 when the imaginary shit i'm writing went down or could be 30 may 2017 when i wrote it down or today could be 16 august 2017 when i'm fine-toothcombing or february

28 going over jim's copyedit or the reader reading this thinking. today as some later date if. at all that reader is less than likely to be diNO even though i'm laying this down for him diNO is my audience diNO gobbled up by the penile system we are all one tiny step from being swallowed up by that system gobbled erased as in he appeared to be resisting we shot him twice in the face the lesson of ausc-witz kharlamov's ankle

scene thirty-nine HANGZHOU *in the powdered boudoir. count the passing days. but in my former life. i saw you in a garden dream. willow sprig in hand. and on your lips. a plea for a poem from me* he waited 1 man alone in his cell for 2 days until he was visited by 3 mice from the kanadian embassy the lead mouse informed him that his country's government presently preoccupied. by the race to win another 4 years in power as a springboard to a further 4 years in power following that was doing everything possible to bring him home he should be patient and avoid antagonizing his hosts when he asked about sheldon epp and claire nomi after a moment's hesitation the mouse explained they had both been transferred out of china finally the mouse cleared its throat aside from miss nomi and mr epp the mouse reminded nik you did not discuss the invitation addressed to huBO or its contents with. anyone at the embassy and am i corrrect in saying that at no time did anyone at the embassy other than those two individuals contact you to discuss the contents of said letter before or after you delivered it to huBO nik's heart sank which when it happens to you is not. merely metaphorical nik said i suppose you're going to ask me to sign something to that effect well the mouse. replied as a matter of fact one of the other mice produced a pen and a sheet of paper containing an eight-line declaration to that effect the mouse turned away and offered its shiny back as a surface upon which nik could sign his name on the ninth line of the statement the mice then took

heaven is unconcerned
and unmindful but its
retribution is ingenious
and beyond the reach
of human plans it is not
necessary to kill evildoers
heaven will do it for us

吴承恩

themselves and his statement away leaving nik alone with the lingering scent of mouse until less than ten minutes later claire appeared in the cell's doorway

scene forty IN SEARCH OF THE MASTER *when did you leave him. do you know the trouble he's got into* i can't stay long she said they were standing in his cell neither wanting or daring to sit on the cot they're sending me away she said moving closer studying him trying to guess what he was thinking nik standing silent his face a mask finally she reached for his hand they haven't hurt you she said have they he shrugged shook his head no not the way. you mean she turned her head looking away absorbing the blow they're shipping me back home she told him yes that'll be hard for you he said being away from chiNa she shook her head made a sweeping gesture with her hand i don't care about that she said epp says they won't keep you long it's just their way of making a statement we interfered in their internal affairs he slipped his hand out of her grasp right he said the invitation she made a quick grab to take back his hand catching hold of his wrist instead listen nik i had no idea about that epp must have slipped it into the pile what was he thinking she said more to herself than to him putting something like that in writing you have to believe me nik i had nothing to do with it nik turned to the small barred window high in the wall that's why you brought me over in the first place to get to huBO to get to his friend all that talk about cultural exchange the concert the music that was just a smokescreen i was your way in she took a step back that's not true she said i met huBO at the opera that's when i got the idea to bring a countertenor over the other stuff that came after that was not my idea but you knew he said you and epp. had it planned

because we are merely travellers stopping now at this inn now at that all of us governed by the things we know the things we happen to encounter but not those that we have never encountered we know how to do the things we can do but we can't do the things we don't know how to do...

before i came and after all that time taking me out showing me the sights she sat down on the edge of the cot it wasn't like that i had the idea for the two high voices at first the ambassador wasn't willing to fund it then epp took a closer look at huBO saw an opening came up with his little scheme all i cared about was the music nik shook his head but you went along with it yes she said softly for the money. well how else was i going to get the money to do it do you really think the embassy gives a shit about culture chinA is just big business to them i'm alone out here i know how you feel nik said turning back from the window they stood a moment in silence nik closing his eyes going over it all in his head then opening his eyes squinting the only way he could look into her face flushed with betrayal you could have told me he whispered claire slumped on the edge. of the cot her head bending over her knees i didn't want to distract you to ruin it for you she broke off then in a low voice later. after. i guess i was ashamed oh nik i'm so sorry he said nothing he couldn't speak his throat. had closed down the cell was suddenly too small to contain the two of them and all the riot of emotions he was waiting for her to leave already alone his world reduced to this cell still she didn't get up sat hunched over her knees as though she were suffering from stomach cramp what happened. between us she said that wasn't part of the plan that was real when he didn't respond she stood up nik she said do you believe me he shrugged it doesn't matter he said she took a deep breath okay listen i'm going to get you out of here i know people in foreign affairs is there someone back home i can get in touch with for you he smiled thinking of his musician friends entirely consumed by their instruments and mostly cut off from the world outside music it occurred to him in

...not to know not to be able to do from these humankind can never escape and yet there are those who struggle to escape from the inescapable — pity them — perfect speech is the abandonment of speech perfect action is the abandonment of action

*庄子 kNOwlEdge wAndeRed nOrtH*

the cutthroat world. of classical music his disappearance would be good news to one or two countertenors never mind he told her if you're right i'll be back there before they could do anything for me their parting was awkward claire in the end settling for squeezing his forearm and tapping her forehead against his once she was gone and the cell door shut he felt a strange kind of relief his first experience of time standing absolutely still a state of being he would need to cultivate

outside the 21cLub on 52nd and 5th ave the goldilocks mafia arrives — in 16 limos SS dicks fanning out to set up a perimeter — goldilocks goes in with trophy daughter et al to standing applause from the big money scarfing up the 21cLub special — don't worry folks goldilocks tells them we'll get your taxes down — strange pair comes in behind them liTTle jiMMy liTTle & emIly dIckInson — emiLy all in black high ruffled collar long black dress towering over wee jiMMy liTTle in a monkey suit he took off a monkey on 42nd street — they get the standard SS frisk then high step it inside — walking past the bar to the tables littLe jImmy littLe says figures goldilocks likes this place — all red & gold & mirrors with the big plush chairs — goldilocks is holding court over a 36US$ hamburger and a bloodied virgin — meanwhile the moneybags are busy taking iphotos and posting ivideos — so that it shouldn't be too tough for light-fingered lIttLe jiMMy liTTle to lift a steak knife & pass off to emIly slasH dIckInson — not — easier for a humpback on legs to pass through the eye of a needle than it is to take a dime or for that matter anything at all including a knife from those rich bastards up on the east side — that little monkey in a monkey suit stole my knife a well-upholstered matron in pearls and yVes saInt lOuiE — what brings the SS dicks down hard on emIly and liTTle jiMMy liTTle cracking jimmy's head in two little pieces — busting emIly dIckinSon's stanza once and for all

and a thousand generations
from now it will still be with us
a thousand generations from
now mark my words there
will be men who will eat each
other up

庄子

emiLy caRR rode the train down to flORida with the dog she called biLLie the cockatoo she'd named saLLie and the parrot. who'd named herself jaNe. she left woo the monkey behind figured he'd draw attention her & billie & sallie & jane rode the rails down to wesT palM beach station across taMarind and down datuRA to the ocean four pals crossed the rOYal pARk bRiDge to pALm bEAch iSland along rOYal pALm wAy to the beach palm trees golf green lawns white sand turquoise sea plenty of security on the bridge & on the island some of it local some federal short story the man was crawling all over the place sure those pigs eyed the old lady and her pets but there's always a few kooks in among the rich eccentric millionaires is what they call them the SS figured emiLy C for one of those the dog barked but they let the caravan pass old lady black headband long loose dress cockatoo sitting pretty on one shoulder parrot on the other billIe bopping longside down the stretch of white sand along oCEAn blvd under blue sky yellow sun billie & emily tongue lolling not used to the heat but sallie and jane're loving it

keep the body whole cling fast to life do not fall prey to the fidget and fuss of thoughts and scheming if you do this for three years then you can attain the state of which i have spoken

庄子

scene forty-one DELAYED EXAMINATION *which is the most appropriate of the three possible policies: attack defence or appeasement* a bowl of porridge occasionally rice and a vegetable sometimes bok choy sometimes beans but mostly green onions to keep the digestive tract busy and the mind off the hunger twice a day in the afternoon he was allowed an hour alone. in the cobbled inner courtyard he did not mind the solitude if he exercised his vocal chords it was not in anticipation of release and return to a career but simply because it was something he knew how to do he did not imagine he had an audience because he heard nothing from the neighbouring cells if there were neighbouring cells slowly day by day gobbling his meagre diet in the damp cell he felt his voice dwindling a small ball of dust in the corner of his cell floats on a faint air current along the stone floor an inch to the wall one side of the corner then back to the wall the other side one morning a kind of silverfish appears on the floor by the ball of dust the insect chases lunges attacks taking barely perceptible bites out of the dustball watching that silverfish work the world gradually reduced to a tiny dustball in the corner of a cell in the peoPle's rePublic of cHina on the continent of asiA

scene forty-two TROOP TRANSFER *in vain we long for the brocade river of our home. and yangzhou's delights are nowhere to be found. stroking your sword judging past and present. how can you bear the idleness of waiting. old and useless i hesitate here still* after claire's visit he ceased marking the days the prisoner who counts the days lives in hope of rejoining the world outside he or she wants to return to that world equipped with a calendar if nothing else nik cast out that hope occasionally he sang in his weakening voice the dust in his throat but he did not talk to himself i mean he constantly talked to himself but not out loud he knew in his solitude he was gradually evolving into something desolate until one afternoon or shall we say THEN and introduce a minor plot point the other westerner in qinCheng was an ameriKan named daVid meKham he exercised it. turned out in the yard adjacent to nik's heard the latter's high voice singing from the other side of the wall and having benefited from a higher education recognized the composer john doWlaNd responded in his own croaky tenor this went on for several weeks until after a very long & very mean while their jailers allowed meKham to join nik for an hour a day in the latter's courtyard meKham the reader may learn by looking over nik morgan's shoulder

Qu'est-ce que l'on vous ferait
en pareil cas si l'on vous
découvrait?
Rien! (il éclate de rire) rien:
je suis européen
C'est vrai mais véritablement
il faut bien que cette nuit
ce soit lui-même qui me le
rappelle c'est vrai ceci explique
et sauve tout: il est européen!

victor segalen *rené leys*

was an overeducated art collector who'd been accused of plundering chinese artifacts and smuggling them out of the country naturally like nik he also chimed his innocence nor was his embassy doing much of anything to get him out our embassy staff are in touch. with the appropriate officials and actively seeking your release it took a while to learn all this because after so many months in solitude both men had lost most of their social skills and furthermore walking circles in the exercise yard with meKham nik was acutely conscious of the gaze of the chinese guards perched up on the walls above whereas the latter had grown accustomed to a solitary westerner pacing in the exercise yard they seemed to be watching the interaction of the two white men with renewed interest the way biologists might study two exotic creatures having placed them together in an enclosure will they mate or will one eat the other

breath

okay here's the plan emily tells jaNe them strolling down the beach close to mar-A-lago jane all decked out in red yellow'n'green you'll carry the spell over the wall emily tells the parrot and straight to goldilocks which is how you'll know him you find the bastard zero. in drop the spell in his lap along with a splash of your parrot shit if you feel the urge then drive your blade-sharp beak straight in his eye the right eye preferably jaNe is up for it no question flaps her wings liftoff from emiLy caRR's shoulder so much of canlit rests on emIly caRR's shoulders like a parrot couldn't we do like jaNe flap our wings & lift up and away where we can do some real damage

scene forty-three THE SIEGE OF HUAIAN *how may we now do like liu kun of ancient qin. by whistling from a moonlit tower. fill these barbarians with thoughts of home* occasionally he was taken from his cell to a larger room to stand before three interrogators dressed in drab khaki zhȯngshan suits and seated behind a long wooden table they listened politely while he repeated his denial of any knowledge of the contents of the letter he had delivered to huBO nik could not tell if they understood engLish he repeated his plea anyway then one of the interrogators would give the order and nik was returned to his cell eventually many months later morgan was granted an audience with warden 阎王 yanWang a tall thin elderly man in a green military uniform sporting a crewcut and thick round eyeglasses who met niK at the door motioned the prisoner to sit on a wooden chair the first chair nik had sat on since his imprisonment yanWang too sat but on the powerful side of the desk before nik could launch into his long nurtured questions the warden told him in excellent engLish you most probably want to know how much longer you are to remain here unfortunately i cannot say i know that discussions have been undertaken with your government more than that i cannot say if you would be willing to compose a brief statement regarding your role in the attempted blackmail of a member of the governing body of the people's rEpuBliC of cHinA i believe that would greatly contribute to your early release i've explained many times nik told him i had no knowledge of the contents of that letter here a reader if such a thing existed might say these are the pencil shavings of the espionage genre and could easily be dispensed with the warden may have agreed he cut him. off with a wave of the hand good good he said in the meantime do you have any special requests i'd like to study your language nik told him it would be something to keep my mind busy

if we were wise we would not fill our lessons with words or our shelves with books

老子

bin a wile since she flew so free & far the air current's upward thrust on her wings the ground falling away below jane aiming first toward the litigated flagpole the palm beach municipality sued goldilocks countersued now it stands 70 feet high down from the original 80 goldilocks' finger in the face of the paLm bEAch set jane wings it across the open field between the road and the pole eye on the flag high-flying with the old man's spell tight in her sharp beak this is as far as she's flown for years over the grassy field she spots the shadow on the ground below too late a wide-winged aMeriKaN eagle circling high its shadow on the ground merging with hers and that any parrot knows is bad news the ameriKan b-29 superfortress claws extended dropping straight down on jaNe her small red head bobbing yellow belly green wings flapping her psittacine hooked beak powerless bye-bye jane

scene forty-four CONCERN FOR THE BESIEGED *tell him how officers of celestial court. by chance discovered. the due fruition of a predestined match. and hastened to open my grave* the guards bring in a low table the elderly monk who calls himself 老驴 laoLü old donkey shuffles in short but fit for his age and circumstance slim almost muscular clear-eyed wearing prison blues carrying old newspapers and a brush he sits on the bed beside nik to begin the chinese lesson with brush & water on newspaper perhaps if & when you can draw a proper character we may graduate to ink

人 刀 力 又 口 口 土 夕 大

scene forty-five A SPY FOR THE REBELS *tranquil post in nanAn. respectable living now lost. it isn't hard to make your fortune. just teach for a thousand years* we should be out soon mekham tells nik deng xiaoping's opening up china he wants good relations with the western powers one way or the other he's bound to send us home *what heaven dislikes who knows the reason the way of heaven is to win without a fight to answer without a word to come without a summons and to plan without a thought*

scene forty-six THE REBELS COUNTERED *awaiting relief we array our troops. in wind and cloud formations. here at the border. a month creeps by like a year. still let the waves of your magnanimity. wash this poor stranded fish* david mekham was half right about deng xiaoPing i'm out in a couple of days he told nik great news nik said i'll miss our morning exercise but i'm truly happy for you mekham clapped him on the shoulder not to worry he said you'll be out soon i'll cross over to kanada we'll have a drink on a terrace overlooking lake ontario but deng xiaoPing did not send nik morgan home why. became clearer months later at nik morgan's second summons to warden yanWang's office by this time nik had a few clumsy sentences of mAndArIn and he could paint a hundred awkward characters he imagined the purpose of warden yanWang's summons was to announce nik's release and he felt a tinge of affection for the warden something the prisoner can afford standing in the open door of his or her cell but when he entered yanWang's office the desk was unmanned no sign of the warden instead standing by the window off to the right. an elderly party cadre wearing a dark blue silk zhongshan jacket thick stylish glasses hair dyed maybe even a toupee a sure sign he was high up in the nomenklatura did not introduce himself i think he said struggling with english you wonder how much longer you are here please sit nik sat the dark blue zhongshan took two steps to lean over nik's shoulder & lay an index. finger on a sheet of paper on the edge of the desk a silver fountain pen lay beside it there is some confusion regarding events during your time as guest of pEopLe'S rePubLiC of chIna perhaps you wish to sign this it will shorten your stay the document was bilingual in chinese first then in english below i nikolas morgan guest of the pEopLe's rEpuBlic of cHiNa wish to thank the government and people of the pEopLe's rEpuBlic of cHinA for the fair and generous treatment i have received in spite of my participation in acts of espionage blackmail and calumny i also wish to refute and deny any rumours of illicit relations involving members of the chinese government rumours which i attempted to propagate in collusion with foreign entities our scandal-mongering and defamation was entirely without foundation the document went on for a bit longer as such documents are wont to do but that's the gist of it no need to waste more ink assuming we have graduated from water

we reward daring
ostentation and progress
meanwhile we praise
patience frugality and
humility in reality we know
these are useless

老子

to ink except to say the fountain pen was a legendary piLOt muReX google that!

女 子 寸 小 工 幺 弓

may 25 aMeriKan airstrikes kill 106 civilians in al maYaDeen sYriA the F-35 liGhTning II (JSF) is worth a potential $200 billion to loCkheed maRtin (total sales 2008 $36 billion) because the changed nature of war no longer disrupts the citizens of the aggressor nations no rationing conscripting or blitzing we continue our daily commute excuse me while i make another buck bobby 2sneakers dug up a couple of yarmulkes he'd kept for no reason stashed away with socks and underwear after his parents kicked him into the street he & curly joe stocked up on mars bars and water bottles headed down to the old port snuck past those slumbering security guards climbed up onto a beatup scrap heap flying a panamanian flAg of convenience slipped under the tarp of a lifeboat & settled in for the long. sea. voyage which we'll skip who needs all that dirty water except to say they were discovered on the third day on account of curly joe kept coming out of hiding to puke over the side the crew put bobby 2sneakers to work peeling old vegetables in the kitchen curly curled up in a corner below the forward hatch this is the way to the promised land

meanwhile oscar and jake needles set out to try their luck at anDrews field they jacked a triumph scrambler in nEwaRk rode down to mary-had-a-little-land lifted a couple of overalls grabbed a can of kerosene and a dickhead matchbox how they got on the airfield they pulled a kind of bait & switch jake needles the bait goes straight in no iD nothing puffy sleeves on a pink shirt bell bottoms fine shine on midnight hightops highstepping right into the security zone pushing past metal detectors uniforms plainclothes moving fast but cool smiling and whistling mary had a little lamb like there's no reason to panic still all the little piggies do panic they're all over him 3 or 4 porcine pounding his face into the ground twisting his arms back for a good cuffing others busy unholstering iron and walkie talkies hopping up & down meanwhile oscAr making so skinny he's invisible slides right through and onto the tarmac hauling kerosene and dickheads boEing deFenSe sPace & seCuriTy total company revenue in 2016 $94.6 billion

on the tarmac oscar thinking what the fuck am i thinking what can you do with a can of kerosene and a box of matches against a goldilocks wrapped up tight in a fully equipped veeC-25A only goldie ain't safe & sound inside airForCe oNe not yet because oscar & needles know. goldilocks' boarding time they'd stopped to watch the latest dribble we call news in the window of a second-hand electronics cash-and-carry on the east side of waShingTon deeC also copped a couple dime bags of smack neeDLes out of it now his part done oScar's turn to play he's feeling alright the smack still running in his veins not enough to nod but enough so he's feeling no pain he's come a long way to end. up on some tarmac packing a can of k-sene and a box of dickheads this might be a bit late to build up some sympathy for osCaR but better late than later his hair was black straight shoulder-length parted. in the middle his grandparents had come up from cHiLe during the pinoShit years then gone back once they were sure piNosHiT was good & dead & buried & unlikely to rise up from the grave but oscar drifted. away into the streets made his way back north lost most of his spanish and hadn't picked up a whole lot of angLish he didn't need a whole lot of any language really he'd seen no evidence language did much good but he was good for the anKle less uptight less of a radishal a softer edge happy to drift not so much commitment to the ankle's cause tho happy to die for it oh and a truly deep commitment to the dope they shared because oScAr knew the pain of this world is too much to bear

when you succeed
be one with success
when you fail
be one with failure

老子

ok so now everything you always wanted to know about the presidential motorcade free info no extra charge about all you'll learn from this book first the rOutE car black limo rolls onto the tarmac few minutes later here comes the piLot car riding point then a swarm of sWEEpers on buzzers then the leaD car then three beaST limos wrapped in ballistic armour night vision secure telephone & internet also independent air supply so good to go in case of nuclear-biological-chemical attack plus a supply of blood type baSTard then potus that's the piece of turd unipotent scumbag riding in on one of those three beaSTs they call the stageCoach then comes the halFback SUV carrying the secret service detail followed by the watCHtower covered in antennae & domes for electronic defence against remotely detonated devices drones etc then the conTroL vehicle carrying the military commander & the nuclear football then a bunch of support vehicles loaded up with sycophants and more military then the CAT (counter assault teams) motherfucking secreT serviCe commandos all decked out in body armour night vision goggles grenades assault rifles riding in hawKeYe reNeGade black suBurBan SUVS flashing lights then the inTeLligenCe diVisiOn car communicating with all units and intelligence sources then the haZarDous maTeRials miTigaTion uNiT truck then the press vans then the roaDruNNer mobile command and control vehicle a suBurBan with antennae farm and satellite communications dishes all over the roof then the ambulance and the rearguard local police cars & buzzers meanwhile look up look way up the oVerWatch helicopter all this every fucking time that piece of turd unipotent scumbag (potus) wants to go for a spin bill comes to $2500 per minute not counting cost of flying the whole operation city-to-city country-to-country on those big military transport planes

success listens only
to applause
to all else it is deaf

elias canetti

so up against all this firepower here's oScaR alone armed with a can of kero and a box of dickhead. matches let's consider his options who wouldn't standing. on that tarmac faced with a presidential tornado take a moment to consider oScar figures here's as good a place as any to drop that penny clenched between his knees anyway he's worn out from the long trip down to waShingTon the shit. in his veins's wearing thin fuck it he's kHarLaMov's anKle he tips. the can of k-sene over his head flicks a dickhead and runs howling la muerta los patrones straight for goldilocks or as close as he can get before the SS boys extinguish our pal our fire-breathing oScar shifted into the past tense

scene forty-seven RAISING THE SIEGE *oh dear oh dear. arms of war shield and spear close-locked. and me here between them* nik did not take up the piLoT murEx pen was he too self-righteous or stubborn or foolish to admit to something he hadn't done of course it occurred. to him that the official standing. beside him in that dark silk zhongshan with a manicured finger on the document was also the one who occasionally dispatched that dark limo. to collect huBO it was likely nik figured since the man would want to involve the fewest possible people in resolving his dilemma which also explained the warden's expulsion from his own office how. powerful was this man how. desperate on his way out the silk-clad official turned at the door reflect on your situation he said back in his cell nIk sat a while on his cot there was no way for him to guess the possible outcome of infighting within the chInEsE leadership and therefore no way to know the right way to go sign the silky comrade's paper. and the comrade might order nik's release but with or without nik's complicity the comrade's scandal might bring him down in which case signing the paper would put nik on the wrong side of history not to mention prematurely putting an end to this particular narrative trajectory he tried to halt or at least slow that narrative's inexorable progress toward disaster in his solitude he sang a little to himself johann schein's psalm 25 turn to me reader and be gracious to me. for i am alone and afflicted. my heart is greatly troubled. bring me out of my distress. behold my affliction and my pain. and forgive all my scribbling.

水 火 木 金 土

scene forty-eight MOTHER AND DAUGHTER REUNITED *when i think of years in a cold grave. rather this glimpse of stars through tattered blinds. than blackness underground* nik morgan's third visit to warden yanWang's office came a few days later this time the wArDen was waiting. behind his desk sipping tea from a small porcelain cup he motioned nik to sit and poured tea into a second cup wulong he told nik of the tieguanyin variety how do you call it in enGlish iron buddha tea from the province of fujian my own home province you are well he asked your manDarin is progressing good good they were silent a moment sipping then yanWang straightened in his chair signalling the end of small talk we have a great number of prisoners here he said some whose crimes were very serious one of these has requested to meet with you until now she has been denied visitors and left to herself but she is ill and can do no further. harm to anyone in her early life this prisoner was active in the cultural domain for a time a performer like you perhaps you have some things in common you may find her. interesting if you agree we can arrange for you to meet and provide a translator nik nodded i think i can fit her into my busy schedule he said the warden smiled good good well perhaps i can help you with some small advice in return regarding your last visit here the comrade you spoke to in this office nik said nothing leaned forward on his chair held his breath and so shall we when we hold our breath we hold it in a pair of hands we call lungs

poverty is a virtue which one can teach oneself

Διογένης ὁ Κυνικός (diogenes the cynic)

hold that breath

scene forty-nine MOORED BEFORE HUAIAN *no easy road to take. in time of strife and disintegration. alas for this simple scholar. helpless before life's hardships. no other occupation. than the struggle with poverty. ah how the breath of autumn speaks. of failure yet to establish name or rank. do not look back. for equal melancholy reigns. south as north of the river* the comrade whom you met in this office some days ago may have suggested an arrangement of sorts warden yanWang said perhaps he requested you sign a document nik dipped his head barely a nod unsure where the warden was heading and how closely nik should follow good

good yanWang said the comrade has spoken to me asked me to assist you in your decision it is probable that he will return very soon to speak with you again if i sign the document nik asked what guarantee do i have that i will be released the warden rose from his chair stepped to the window turning his back to nik for a few long moments then he took a deep breath seemed to make a decision good good he walked back to the desk poured more tea into those tiny cups that seemed to contain all nik's hopes the warden sat down the situation he said is somewhat complicated it is as you say in flux. changing nik lay his cup carefully back on the tray then why would i sign the document he said yanWang leaned forward nodded yes why would you he said nik leaned closer across the desk yanWang his voice barely audible whispered if you sign that document morgan xiansheng i am doubtful it will guarantee your release in fact the outcome could be quite the reverse nik drew back in his chair you're telling me not to sign the document the warden gesture for nik to lower his voice these are matters that concern the leadership of the pArTy mister morgan they do not concern us he said they concern me nik said i'm damned concerned yanWang nodded of course of course however regardless of the outcome within the leadership let us simply say for the time being it is advisable not to sign anything the two men sat in silence waiting for the charged air in the room to settle

in a rich man's house
there is no place to spit
but in his face

Διογένης ὁ Κυνικός

谢谢 阎王 师傅

scene fifty UPROAR AT THE BANQUET *injustice oh my wife my wife. for love of fondling jade i aspired. to join the noble house of qiN. but now must copy zhongYi in scholar's hat. prisoner from the land of cHU* they met in a room not much bigger than his cell but furnished with wooden chairs and a small table upon which a grey metal thermos of hot water and two glasses had been placed the guard who had accompanied nik to the meeting remained inside at the door a young male translator was standing at one end of the table she was seated on one of the chairs facing the door she wore a grey prison uniform identical to his her hair was cut short they had taken her glasses nik sat down facing her and the blue sky framed in the barred window high on the wall behind her of course i do not deny the beauty. and power of some western dramatic art works shakesPeare ibSen moLière goetHe breCht we too have many dramatic masterpieces in our long history the peoNy paViLion for example but what good do these works do for the overwhelming majority of humanity who. benefits from their production who is your audience when you yourself perform for wealthy patrons in evening dress black tails mink coats precious jewels who experience a gratifying catharsis and leave the theatre smug self-satisfied having confirmed their value as elite consumers of high culture then home to a sumptuous meal soft beds precious homes we tried to create a theatre for the people something to inspire to foster. fearless courage in the struggle against their exploiters for real equality and justice yes the peOny paVilion is a work of genius the highest degree of artistic merit the language poetic technique the sophisticated critique of social hypocrisy sexual repression woman's oppression success is measured by achievement of a higher status for the male and marriage for the woman all nicely wrapped in the sweet treacle of love alright you are thinking but 8 plays is not a lot for all those masses of people we want to reach well it was a start first we had to purge the country of all the bourgeois treacle then to create truly revolutionary works we were starting from scratch experimenting discovering new forms rooted in our chinese traditions and in proletarian and peasant experience in any case by the time of denG xiAoPing's counterrevolutionary coup there were many more than 8. operas those who attack us never mention that yes that's right i said counterrevolutionary coup who. really suffered during our cultural revolution the rich the privileged the intellectuals and academics unfortunately the proletariat and peasants have neither the time nor the means to defend themselves in the international media in longwinded volumes pretty poems the peasants and workers do not write columns in the newspapers they do not share cocktails in the halls of justice rub elbows with the rich and powerful because as we know even after they are defeated the ruling classes continue to represent a threat to the revolution they have the skills the training the resources and the international backing to regain power and not only by military means but what's more dangerous by infiltrating the revolution worming their way back into power through the organs of the state and the economic institutions cHairMan mAo believed. it would take 8 generations to consolidate the revolution to disarm the old ruling class and to provide the workers and peasants with the means and skills necessary to run a country we were not given 8 generations barely 2 did we oppress a great number of intellectuals and bourgeois elements yes we did did we kill a number of them yes but clearly we did not kill enough of them after all here i am and that little rat deng xiaoping is in zhongNanHai they portray me as a barbarian ignorant provincial but that is false i can i do appreciate your art I prefer. william byrd over john dowland i find dowland too sentimental too full of self-pity of course my problem with baroque is the polyphony the contending voices the masses require a single united voice not these multiple voices intertwined of course you can't agree the baroque being your terrain and you may be right cHaiRmAn mAo said let a hundred flowers bloom however he did not suggest we let a hundred weeds run rampant if you. merely pluck the weed it will soon grow back weeds. must be attacked at the root she stopped. took a deep breath he could see her long diatribe had exhausted her she sipped from the glass of warm water the translator stood up indicating their meeting was coming to an end slowly she pulled herself out of her chair perhaps if we are given the opportunity to talk again she said to nik before you leave us you would sing for me i would enjoy that very much nik shrugged oh i don't think i'm going anywhere

learn to condemn light
happy happy they that in hell
feel not the world's despite

john dowland

for a while this surprised her a moment of silence a tilt of the head tell me she said and he did the whole crazy story through the translator when he was done she stood in silence a moment her hands steepled on the tip of her chin finally she nodded leaned forward and spoke directly to him in engLish we have expression in chinese 進退維谷 *jin tui wei gu* you may go forward you may retreat but no matter you are caught in a valley the man who came to see you is almost certainly du bAo a member of politburo that is highest body in the parTy he is advocate of socialism not a follower of deng xiaoping's reactionary capitalist program so a rival to be destroyed by any means his unfortunate sexual appetites his relationship with performer huBO that is his weak spot which deng xiaoping will seek to exploit do you understand yes nik said one side wants me to quash the rumours the other wants to use them what should i do she shrugged when to advance and to retreat are equally dangerous one should how do you say it stay put yes? nik nodded yes stay. put she smiled proud of her engLish you must wait to see who triumphs in central committee the translator put a hand gently on her elbow she nodded now i must rest she said the guard spoke through the door it swung open and she shuffled out of the cell she'd spoken almost without pause the entire time allotted to them even the translator looked exhausted nik could see that after her long isolation she needed to talk but more than that he could see in her need to talk the bitterness of someone who has been defeated knowing or at least convinced she had been in the right also he could see she was. ill whether from the long detention what they'd done to her or something more serious he doubted he would see her. again no matter how long they kept him which was a pity because in spite of everything he would have liked to sing for her if only to provide a brief moment of release in which she could have escaped her self

our poetry now is the
realization that we
possess nothing

john cage

为无为　道可道

breath

breath

breath

they picked up a couple of raggedy black business suits with that low ranking rabbinical waxed look at the sally ann & took the bus to the foot of yaFO street gritted their teeth hoofed it slowly up. yaFO to the tourist info grabbed a tourist map then slogged onto oMar beN el-Hatab and stone stairs up to daViD street they got. a good shove & elbows workover in the narrow passage through the bazaar good news though the lOrd provideth

n'était-ce pas là-bas dans l'extrême détresse qui n'est même pas celle de quelqu'un que m'avait été offert le droit de parler de moi à la troisième personne

maurice blanchot

a kid. came on to them maybe 10 yrs old small dark wiry little pissface sold them a couple caps of smack and a dropper with an old blunt 25 point needle scotch-taped on the end not pretty and a hassle. hitting the vein like ramming a camel. through the eye of a needle biblical reference not to mention bug risk but so what at this point bobby 2sneakers picked up a couple of old tattered laces to tighten his tattered sneakers ready for action then more. twists & turns more stairs to ha-KoTeL street more twists to baTeI mahaSSe then here comes the last bit more stairs and bingo we're on the sand-colo(u)red stone. plaza the israeli boy and girl. soldiers already clearing everyone out for the incoming motorcade we were the aNkle we did a quick slide into a mess. c'est le cas de le dire. of scaffolding north side of the plaza they're always renovating historical sites not to mention history ducked under some tarp put our yarmulkes right did the needlework & settled in for a meet & greet riding the dope neither of them. had ever diddled with the religion they were born. into matter fact after he'd been tossed out the nest bobby 2sneakers'd pretty much forgotten his judaeanness later on after he'd been reminded of it once or twice those christians will. do that once he'd run up face-first again & against. that not so gentle gentile wall they shove up against the people of the book he'd tattooed A5591 and 61991 on his arm still he did not return to the fold not that the folded would have taken him back those folks in the fold were no gentler than the gentiles he was. apikoros l'israel n'est pas en israel still once in that stAte apart and apartheid he'd hidden those tattoos for one thing the biblical taboo on tattoos. not to mention track marks ever since that old kiNg yeHoiaKim tattooed the name of god on his organ i mean his dick he was not musical go ahead look it up sanHeDrin tract of the babyLonian talmud in any case the good citizens of zion did not enjoy being reminded of their past victimization even when they were climbing the stony road to the place of weePing which the people of paleStiNe. let's not forget them it's their road too. call el-Mabka

reasons why we hate shakesPeare: frailty thy name is woman

scene fifty-one THE LIST PROCLAIMED *speak not of cares of office. nor of old age hastening on. when there in cHamBer couRt he stands. in solitary dignity.* what do you call a situation that is an impasse a stalemate a deadlock while that friend of huBO in a black limo tugged on one of nik morgan's arms and his comrades in the politburo tugged on the other time passed and then passed away when time passes timelessness is all that remains only the circling hours of day wake up a bowl of congee. once he learned to speak the language well enough to understand commands they put him to work. in the laundry lunch a bowl of rice then more work in the laundry mandarin study with laO lü exercise in the yard bowl of rice lights out the long loopy circles of night there was no counting how many such circles passed because there was no end to the circling he learned to live with that to live like that something laO lü taught him along with the chinese radicals i mean the characters not the gang of four he learned to dream the same dream every night a small pond like the one at the embassy lotus pads pink and white flowers afloat in one corner their long stems anchored by roots in the deep silent water below and the fish a handful of ordinary grass goldfish some fantail and a pair of dragon eye suspended or slow moving in the intermediate world of the pond here the reader if there was one might reread this paragraph over and over again for a while thereby reproducing in some small way niK moRgan's time in qinCheng prison

非常道

scene fifty-two THE SEARCH FOR THE CANDIDATE *would you believe it he makes prize candidate and doesn't even care. can you credit it. makes prize candidate and stirs up all this fuss. can you imagine makes prize candidate and off he trots who'd have thought it he makes prize candidate and disappears* one afternoon laO lü entered nik's cell with ink stick and stone you are ready to blacken your fingers he said

金鱼

here for the sake of argument an argument for letting it be leaving it alone if the gentleman can in truth keep from rending apart his five vital organs from tearing out his eyesight and hearing then he will command corpse-like stillness and dragon vision the silence of deep pools and the voice of thunder his spirit will move in the train of hEaVEn gentle and easy in inaction and the ten thousand things will be dust on the wind what leisure have I now for governing the world like bartLebY he will say iamwritingiamwritingiamwriting

scene fifty-three INTERROGATION UNDER THE ROD *the criminal liU mengMei for opening of coffin and theft of contents sentenced to be beheaded when this has been drawn up let it be presented to the convicted party and have him sign below the word beheaded completed document to be placed on file* when they released him it was already the turn of the century grey-haired niKoLaS mOrGaN did not take. the next plane home to kaNada he did not show up at the embassy gates begging for a renewed passport a couple bucks and a ticket home his final lesson with laO lü the old donkey waved away the inkbrush and paper would you do something for me before you go of course if i can nik said sing for me the monk said i'm afraid my worthless voice what little i once had is gone nik told him i can no longer sing laO lü was quiet for a moment you sing for yourself do you not nik laughed yes when i'm alone my voice is very bad the daoist shook his head no matter if your voice is bad i will strive to improve my listening nik shuts his eyes recalls old memories begins to sing the aria of bridaL dU's dream from the peoNy paViliOn as huBO taught him years ago but in the high voice of a euRoPeAn countertenor laO lü shuts his eyes the two men sit blindly face to face *against the weathered rock. he leaned my wilting body. then as he laid my jade limbs down. smoke rose up from jade in the warm sun. by balustrade. past swing. there i spread the folds of my skirt. a covering for the earth. for fear of the eyes of heaven. then it was we knew. perfect mystery. of joy ineffable* what will you do now laO lü asks once silence has gradually refilled the room you will go home to your country nik shrugs don't know there's really nothing for me in that place you could stay a while at the baiYun guan the white cloud temple in beiJing laO lü says it can be a cocoon until you have grown your wings thank you nik says i will gladly go there though i am far too old now to grow wings the old monk smiles once i was too young to grow wings then suddenly i was too old nik accepts this as gentle reprimand when will they release you he asks laO lü shrugs it is of no importance i am content my mind has grown smaller over time to adjust to the smaller space with luck and some hard work perhaps it will disappear altogether

to apply names in the manner of those academics is to invite evil

庄子

first sign of goldilocks the high octane thrum of the presi-dented motorcade limos and sweeper bikes rolling up into the parking area outside the courtyard curly joe blinks away the smack dream rolls an edge of the tarp back turtleheads a sneak peek at the security all decked out in matching suits & ear pods & uzis all over the fucking. plaza says to bobby 2sneakers let's grab a ride & run the bastard down they work their way into the parking lot the sweepers standing around with their heads tucked under their arms smoking dirty jokes with their hands in their pockets diddling their dicks saying how they admire goldilocks his easy access to women meanwhile their bikes curled round their stands cooling curly joe & bobby 2sneakers wade in doing their best raggedy bent rabbinical look which isn't a big stretch religion being opium they've got that pale skinny curved spine down pretty much in israel and not just in israel the curved jew being as invisible as the junkie they hop.

let me explain in dada dada
floats a river around dada
around dada dada dadaizes
dadaizing let this be said for
those who still don't know it
kurt schwitters

the first hog i mean chopper not cop in the row curly joe grabs the bars bobby 2sneakers wrapped up behind him that's how they learned to ride back home back then curly got paid for a key of hash in wheels they'd waited till night shot up a couple vials of morphine they'd copped from a nurse in case of accident curly joe'd kicked. the triumph awake and ground the gears across town down in the shittier part of town riding hard down saInT-anToiNe a kid in pigtails polka dot dress little kiddie strap-on shoes steps off the curb while her mom's busy pram-wrestling curly hits the brakes twists the bike into a sideways skid out from under them stops just short of the frozen kid and the puddle she peed on the road the boys were okay except for bobby 2shoes' scraped elbow & palm of one hand jeans shredded off a leg twisted ankle the cops took them in confiscated the wheels and jammed them up in station 1 for the night anyway that's how curly joe was thereafter designated D but back to the present i mean the present of the story not the present of my writing or the present of your reading we were in the holy land on a US of A pig cycle curly joe kicks the story into gear they whip away leave the ameriKan dickheads and buzzers in the holy dust ride straight at the western wall curly joe bent over the bars bobby 2sneakers one hand wrapped around joe's curly waist the other windmilling the old man's magic spell curly rides the element of surprise right thru the first line of SS pigs onto the plaza they can see goldilocks now a black yarmulke riding on his yellow bird's nest stepping up to the wall his women moving off to the area reserved for their sex that's so god can sort out their gendered prayers by now. all the swine in that holy place koSher & otherwise are woke up and fusterclucking curly joe does some fancy sweaving for a bit the wall. of pigs between the anKle and the wailing wall closing in joe abandons avoidance goes right at them mows down a couple before one pig with brains swings the butt end of his long gun at curly's curls & the bike slides out from under them thereby echoing an earlier narrative digression

scene fifty-four GLAD NEWS *now the dawn suddenly reveals. the gate that leads to heaven* in the white cloud temple they gave him a mat to sleep on an old white cotton shirt and black cotton pants they did not ask him to do anything but after a couple of days watching the monks cleaning toilets preparing meals sweeping he joined in of his own accord he especially enjoyed sweeping the steps of the temple in the courtyard the clear empty sky the sun's warm breath on his face clouds adrift a pale moon working the plough he learned qigong he learned the verb to be mute 哑 pronounced *ya* and the word for nothingness 无 *wu* which is what he sought to achieve he learned to read the 道德经 dao de jing by the philosopher 老子 laozi and then he memorized it he learned the prayers and breathing exercises to attain the ecstasy of nothing and the prayers and exercises to protect the community because in the end those two practices are all you need the temple was a small world but larger than the prison and a way back at once into and out of the world

that chopper & curly joe were unmoved. by the crash i mean they lay motionless in the case of curly joe he would remain. unmoved forever more though later they did move him out of the square and into the coroner's tent where they performed their favourite autopsy tǫ determine the extent of his juDaeaNneSs mean.while bobby 2sneakers one pant. leg shredded an elbow & a palm scraped bloody also twisted aNkle drags himself out from under. the bike up on his other ankle head spinning but opium still working on the pain spots goldilocks in a tight circle of protection a ring of pork i mean lots of not kosher men with guns sirens. wailing in that plaza full of wailing bobby 2sneakers wailing & windmilling the old man's arTaudian spell to strike down the reich chancellor i mean rich chancellor bobby 2sneakers turns from the wall of trigger fingers between him and goldilocks turns on his good ankle makes for the big stone wall instead okay so that catches the pork loins by surprise long enough for bobby 2sneakers to slip the spell in a crack between two stones in that stoned wall before the SS let loose with the proverbial hail of bullets what? proverb is that you may wonder it is the proverb of bullets mentioned earlier goes like this he was unarmed but appeared to be resisting we shot him twice in the face

i wonder if you will become tired and discouraged me i will never give up

gabriel dumont

let's pause briefly here to say catalunya nou estat d'euRopA

scene fifty-five REUNION AT COURT *you buried them in paper coffin. with your own tongue as shovel* blUe took his time worked his way north when he hit. the border told them he was visiting a friend name and address kanAdian customs wants to know blUe picks a name out of the blue norMan betHune he says so this norman lives where customs clown wants to know 1 sussex drive blUe says recalling another of those anKle legends well that gets him over only. he doesn't trek out to no sussex drive not even to that shithole capital city full of desk jockeys in suits instead he drags his ass up to the old man's town east end where the old man's holed up in a room and a half the old man calls my gReY sKiEs tEmPle anyway by this time blUe's long trip north he's wiped and so might the reader be. weary i mean. i know i am and yet here we are at last standing outside the old man's crib hold up a minute blUe can just make out coming from inside the room and a half that high disembodied diplococci angel's voice singing thin but clear notes sans émotion humaine singing *from those boughs which thy winds shake. far from human troubles placed. songs to the lorD would i make. darkness from my mind then take. music all thy sweetness lend. while of his high power i speak. on whom all powers else depend. but my breast is now too weak. trumpets shrill the air should break. all in vain my sounds i raise* the old man's door is open not wide open but nuff so the dog can go if he should ever so desire blUE slow-steps through into a room empty cept for low wooden table tatami mat sink two-ring burner on the counter white walls and the old man upstanding arms extended out to either side eyes shut all loosey goosey and trilling might be at least looks that way to bLue the old man's riding a foot and a half off the ground that could be on account blUe's so wasted he lays his blackpack down settles for a sit & wait in the corner you've come a long way the old man says rustling up hot water & a bite to eat i guess blUe says and i've a long way back scarfing dofu & noodles your shit was weak man he tells the old man we need some real heavy magic man the old man sighs nods sits on the floor beside bluE i think says he there will always be a lot of little hitlers running around ready & able to step up bluE nods sure i get it only we just want a shot at the big bastard the old man shrugs you can stay here a while if you like blUe shakes his head no man i gotta finish this thing the old man nods rises a little stiffly all that free-floating feeling gone fetches a sheet of old yellowing news an inkstick inkstone & a medium-sized mouse-hair brush takes a deep breath draws a line through the newspaper headline sAuDi aRaBia buys $14.8 billion of light armoured vehicles from geNeRaL dyNamiCs of kaNaDa the old man dips the brush takes it to the paper and lets it swing through the strokes in easy order chanting the incantation as he writes

not to talk not to be silent this
is the highest form of debate

庄子

following are instructions for creating a talisman to repair damage where calamity has struck and to destroy a ghost devil or human destructor who says literature. teaches us nothing

3 dot strokes on top representing 3 daoist gods. write the character 斗 *dou* (to fight) draw a circle clockwise around the character. where the line intersects with base of the character 斗 draw a long line downward and looping back up to the right. on both the line descending and the loop rising write the character 火 *huo* (fire) stressing the left-curving stroke on the left and the right-curving stroke on the right. from the bottom of the circle where it intersects with 斗 draw five jagged lightning bolts down the middle lifting your brush for each bolt and adding a final dot at the base

while painting the talisman to destroy evil the following incantation must be chanted seven times

| **杳杳冥冥** | ***yǎo yǎo míng míng*** | **dark dark under underworld** |
|---|---|---|
| 天地昏沉 | *tiān dì hūn chén* | heaven & earth confused |
| **雷电风火** | ***léi diàn fēng huǒ*** | **thunder lightning wind fire** |
| 官将吏兵 | *guān jiàng lì bīng* | official general officer trooper |
| **若闻关名** | ***ruò wén guān míng*** | **if you hear your rank** |
| 迅速来临 | *xùn sù lái lín* | come quick come fast |
| **驱除幽厉** | ***qū chú yōu lì*** | **drive out dark calamity** |
| 拿捉精灵 | *ná zhuō jīng líng* | grasp your essential spirit |
| **安龙镇宅** | ***ān lóng zhèn zhái*** | **conquer dragons destroy home** |
| 功在天庭 | *gōng zài tiān tíng* | so to attain heaven |

so you figure this is gonna do it says blUe leaning hard on the skeptical the old man busy scrubbing brush & inkstone if you can get him to swallow it he says that would be best

reasons why we hate shakespeare: iambic pentameter

blUe in beige coveralls going up in the golden tromperie tower's golden elevator armed with nothing. but a talisman figures shit this be one time i get upwardly mobile on a one-way ticket get a leg up on this gangsters' level 58th floor. penthouse from up there a boy could piss all over nu jack & clear across to jerky well at this point let's hold up. the narrative so we're all in the elevator going up carrying the old man's talisman in one hand all eyes on the panel the white light climbing tromperie is it crowded in there with blUe and the author & all the readers no certainly not crowded and yet not yet because here's the paradox of our dilemma a story about real people who never had the weapons to tell their story addressed not to the people who read stories about people who are denied the power to tell their own stories but to those very people who will never read this story to diNO and mike wIrth who we sometimes called reD to juDy juDy who had to wait for her share of the dope to jaKe needles who dressed cool and ripped fine to little jimmy little who maybe got capped in a rip or hung his own ass kill the memory of doing time up in bordEAux penitentiary to oScaR's opium den in the basement of the frat house on pEEL to curly jOe who figured out you can't beat the house but you can play for a draw to idjit and bobby 2shoes who were really one very stupid person and also to emIly diCkinSon who slashed the throat of language to emIly caRr who heard the wail of a dying tree long before anyone gave a shit to both emIlys in spite of all the crap they teach us about those women in skool to jane a parrot who named herself and to the dog we called him uGo that taught the old man how to live inside and outside the world let's step away from the story and consider one or two outstanding questions will blUe deliver the letter the sooner the better will he put an end to the tromperie or will blUe turn on the author don't put your load on me man i'm not your mailman carry your own letters these questions left hanging in the elevator shaft above and below us though i admit to weight of apprehension the fear of stopping because writing we are like those obligate ram breather sharks that must keep swimming or die but not the shark in. the anthropocentric world of literature from which i have turned away not the shark as metaphor for powerful predatory ruthless this author being so much less maybe a tiny hummingbird insect-like insignificant hovering at a standstill panicked wings

old man tried to imagine the inner monologue of the dog he said let there be boats and carts but no reason to ride them let people return to the use of knots let there be another state so near people hear its dogs and chickens but live out their lives without making a visit who failed to prepare the fish for the terrible journey which has already begun

breath

a fishbone fish a fefishbone
lay on the on lay on the stone
you may believe the sea has thrown
the fefefishbone there upone

there came a fish a fefe [*whistle*] fisher
a fefefisher came alone
he used to sit while he was fefishing
he uuused to ssit upon this stone

the fisher saw while he was fishing
while he was fishing saw the bone
he took it took he tetetook it
he tetetook it from the stone

now lies the lies now lies the stone
without an out without a bone
and all surrounded by the water
the pepeparn stone is alone

kurt schwitters

## ABOUT THE AUTHOR

Robert Majzels was born in Montréal and holds a Canadian passport, but he'll be damned if he'll stand up for anybody's national anthem. *kHarLaMoV's aNkLe* is his fifth novel. He has also published a play, a book of poetry (with Claire Huot), a number of translations, including five novels by the Acadian writer France Daigle (one of which was awarded a Governor General's Award), and, with Erín Moure, a number of books of poetry by Nicole Brossard (one nominated for the GG in translation and for the Griffin Prize). For seven lean years, he was an associate professor of English and creative writing at the University of Calgary until he walked away in 2015. He now lives somewhere on Vancouver Island in British Columbia, where he writes from time to time, and tries to think otherwise.